Independence Avenue

Independence Avenue

by Eileen Bluestone Sherman

The Jewish Publication Society
Philadelphia - New York
5751 - 1990

This volume is dedicated by
Dr. and Mrs. D. Walter Cohen
in honor of
The Bat Mitzvah of their granddaughter,
Rachel Erin Millner
October 13, 1990   24 Tishri 5751

Copyright © 1990 by Eileen Bluestone Sherman
First edition. All rights reserved.
Manufactured in the United States of America.
Jacket illustration copyright © 1990 by M. Kathryn Smith
Book design by Edith T. Weinberg
The Jewish Publication Society
Philadelphia - New York
5751-1990

Library of Congress Cataloging-in-Publication Data

Sherman, Eileen Bluestone.
    Independence Avenue / Eileen Bluestone Sherman.
       p.   cm.
    Summary: Elias, a fourteen-year-old Russian immigrant, arrives alone in
Kansas City in 1907, finding new employment and friends but also
receiving bad news about his family back in Russia.
    ISBN 0-8276-0367-3 : $13.95
    [1. Russian Americans—Fiction. 2. Emigration and immigration-
Fiction. 3. Jews—Fiction.] I. Title.
PZ7.S54552IN 1990
[Fic]—dc20   90-37662
                                              CIP
                                              AC

To the next generation:
JOSHUA, STEPHANIE, GABRIEL, ROBYN and JENNY

Contents

A Few Still Remember

BETWEEN 1907 AND 1914, a unique historical project called the Galveston Movement brought about ten thousand Jewish immigrants to the West. At its best, life for the immigrant has always been a struggle in America. Yet, during the first part of the twentieth century, the world of Independence Avenue in Kansas City, Missouri, held the promise of a better tomorrow. I will be forever grateful to Abraham Bograd and Harry and Esther Mallin, who graciously invited me into their homes and their childhoods. They still remember Jacob Billikopf, the Settlement House, peddlers hawking wares from their wagons, outhouses, shows at the Pantages Theater, newsboys on street-corners, men's garters, and trolley rides for a nickel. They also remember poverty, the label "greenhorn," and a fierce determination to secure a better life.

One other friend must be acknowledged. Robert Rosenwald, of blessed memory, devoted a lifetime to charitable organizations in his hometown of Kansas City. He, better than anyone, knew the history of the United Jewish Charities and all that it offered to so many immigrants throughout the years. Through Mr. Rosenwald, I gradually began to understand the outpouring of generosity of the community I now call home. His knowledge and direction were invaluable. I thank his wonderful wife and my dear friend, Dorothy Rosenwald, for bringing us together and continuing to guide me during these last months of writing.

—EBS

Independence Avenue

1

October 29, 1907

ELIAS CHEREVNOSKY OPENED HIS EYES; for a moment he didn't know where he was. Then he saw the porthole and everything came back to him. Suddenly, he remembered something very important about this day and jumped to his feet. By accident he bumped Lieberman who was snoring on the next mattress. The man grunted and turned over on his side. Elias remained very still. Today of all days he did not want Morton Lieberman to wake up any earlier than necessary.

The snoring continued and Elias sighed gratefully. Quickly he buttoned his jacket and turned to go outside. Then he remembered his scarf, still folded neatly on his mattress. Elias used it as a pillow at night, but during the day he kept the scarf wrapped around his neck. Holding his nose, he carefully tiptoed to the door. The steerage compartment smelled of too many unkempt bodies sleeping side by side. In some cases bodies were even sprawled on top of one another.

He stepped out on deck and took a deep breath. The sky was becoming lighter. Elias knew that within the hour crowds of weary travelers would be congregating on deck, trying to make another tedious day pass as quickly as possible. Even now, a few of the third-class passengers had chosen to curl up on benches outside. Several members of the German crew were already busy at work, but still the deck seemed unusually peaceful.

No one warned us about the miseries of the ship, Elias thought to himself as he took a deep breath of fresh air, but the sea is wonderful! I know Mama and Papa will like it, too. He began to think about his family still in Russia and wondered whether his father was already at his sewing machine in Gomel. He knew his parents would be thinking about him today especially. After all, it was his birthday: October 29, 1907.

"Fourteen years old!" he shouted to a flock of birds flying overhead. Then he remembered his father's warning and nervously looked to see if someone might have overheard him.

"To anyone who asks," Mr. Cherevnosky had instructed his son, "you say you are seventeen. With your build, no one will doubt you."

All his life Elias had heard how "big" he looked for his age. Secretly, he had always hated it when relatives exclaimed, "What a big boy!" But now on the ship, he was continually pulling back his shoulders and sticking out his chest to look even larger. He understood that his size was the reason he had earned a free ticket from Gomel, Russia to Galveston, Texas.

"Well, not exactly free," groaned Elias as he thought about his benefactor, Morton Lieberman. When his friends had heard that Elias had agreed to accompany their Hebrew teacher across the Atlantic, they had all pretended to mourn for him.

"A fate worse than death!" they had all shouted. "Even the Czar deserves better."

But Elias had laughed at them. In fact, when Lieberman had first proposed his offer the boy had asked only one question.

"Why me?"

"There's a new program being organized by Jewish leaders in America," the teacher had replied. "Jobs and housing will be waiting for anyone who is willing to sail to a port called Galveston. They promise very high wages, but there are certain requirements. The Americans want young, strong men who have real skills—blacksmiths, shoemakers, carpenters. I notice you are apprenticing with your father. That's fine. They want tailors, too. On the other hand, they have no use for me. What good is an aging, sickly Hebrew teacher? But who will question it, if a devoted nephew travels with his dear, old uncle?"

Elias could not help but smile whenever the short, chubby man referred to his "sickly" condition. As far as anyone knew, Morton Lieberman had never been seriously ill, but he was always complaining. The school boys often poked fun at their hypochondriac teacher.

Jacob Cherevnosky never approved of these jokes. He insisted that Elias be especially kind to this man who had no wife or children. When Mr. Cherevnosky learned about Lieberman's offer, he knew immediately why the teacher had selected his son.

"Lieberman figures you look like a man," he explained to Elias. "That's why you will tell everyone you're seventeen.

Of course, since you're really a boy, he knows you'll stick close to him. Someone older would abandon him once in America. Oh, boychik, without a family, it must be very difficult. At least with you there, Lieberman will have someone. No one wants to be all alone in this world."

Elias looked out toward the horizon. He could still hear the sadness in his father's voice. Since leaving Gomel, he had understood all too well what it meant to be alone. According to his father's plan, the family would be together within a year, but at that moment, twelve months seemed like a lifetime.

He didn't have very long to stand there and feel sorry for himself. He heard a woman's cry and automatically turned toward the sound. All he saw were two sailors huddling in a corner. Elias walked closer and heard the men laughing.

"Come on. You'll be in America soon. You don't need that rag on your pretty head," one was teasing.

"I am a married woman. It is our custom to cut our hair and keep our heads covered."

"Take it off!" the other coaxed. "The breeze feels good."

"It's obvious she doesn't want to take it off!" Elias said just loud enough to make his presence known. The men turned and faced Elias. One was slight and not much bigger than the trembling woman, but the other stood head to head with the fourteen-year-old and looked him straight in the eye. "I thought you people were cowards," he mocked.

Elias glared at the sailor. The German curled his bottom lip, pretending to look upset.

"Oh," he whined. "I think we hurt the Jew's feelings. We wouldn't want that, now." He looked over at his sidekick and winked. "Karl, I think this passenger needs some special attention." Suddenly, Elias felt a fist pound into his stomach.

The powerful blow unsteadied the boy, and he dropped to his knees.

The young woman gasped in horror. As she leaned forward to help Elias, the smaller sailor grabbed her kerchief off her head. Tears rolled down her cheeks. "Leave us alone," she begged.

The sailor dangled the scarf high in the air and then let it drop into the sea. "Let your hair grow, woman," he shouted. The sailors were still laughing as they turned up the far corner of the deck.

Slowly, Elias pulled himself to his feet.

"Are you all right?" the woman asked.

"Sure," mumbled Elias with a nod. He took off his red scarf and handed it to the woman. "Here, put this on."

"Thank you," she whispered. After tying the scarf on her head, she used one of the ends to pat her wet cheeks. "Those men were animals. Are you sure you're all right?"

"I'm fine," the boy insisted. Elias didn't know which hurt more—the ache in his belly or his bruised pride. He was embarrassed that he had not defended himself better.

"You look very pale," the woman remarked. "I think we should go see the doctor."

"Oh, no!" protested Elias.

Just then a booming voice called out, "There you are!" Elias looked up and saw a stocky, red-bearded young man coming toward him. The man boldly placed his arm around the woman's shoulders.

"I'm sorry, Shlomo," she said. "I woke up very early with the queasy feeling in my stomach again, and I just had to get some fresh air. It's terribly stuffy in the women's quarters. I know we agreed to meet outside the dining room in the mornings, but—"

"Don't be alarmed. Your wife is fine," interrupted Elias.

The woman and man glanced at one another and started laughing. Shlomo's laugh had a deep, booming ring to it and Elias found himself laughing, without knowing why. But he stopped quickly. The jerky movement made his insides hurt even more.

Finally, the woman said, "We're not married."

"I should say not!" said Shlomo with a mischievous grin. "I've known this woman all my life, and I can vouch that she comes from the best of families. But I've got my heart set on an American bride." Elias looked very confused.

"Please excuse us," apologized the woman. "Of course, I am married, but Shlomo is my baby brother. My husband, Yussell, is already in Kansas City."

"Baby!" cried Shlomo with an indignant air. "I'll be eighteen by the time we dock."

"Really? I'm seventeen today!" announced Elias proudly.

Introductions followed. Elias soon learned that Debra Resnick and her brother Shlomo Zusstovetch were Jews from Kiev. "In his letters, my husband tried to prepare me for this journey, but conditions are much worse than I had ever imagined."

While Elias listened politely, he stood with his arms folded across his middle. Shlomo saw him wince a couple times and suspected something was not right.

"Are you sick?" he asked Elias.

The boy quickly shook his head but Debra pleaded once more, "Please, go see the doctor." She turned to her brother and told him about the two sailors.

Shlomo let out a sigh of disgust. "It's just another example of why we must give up some of our old ways if we don't want to be easy targets."

Debra's large brown eyes opened in anger. "We had this discussion before, and I will not grow my hair! It would be disrespectful to my husband. Until we have enough money to buy a beautiful wig, I will wear a kerchief proudly."

"But we're starting new lives. We're being given a second chance. Why must you call attention to yourself?"

Debra put her hands over her ears and squeezed her eyes shut.

"Fine," sighed Shlomo. "Do as you like. As for me, I'm changing my name the moment I step on American soil. What about you, Cherevnosky?"

The question startled Elias. He had never considered the problem. After a moment's hesitation, he shrugged. "I don't know how Papa would feel about it."

"So you've come with your father?" asked Debra, who was eager to change the subject.

When Elias shook his head, Shlomo said, "No one should be alone on his birthday. Come, we'll celebrate the whole day together."

Elias smiled. "Thank you, but I'm not alone. In fact, my uncle is probably having a fit this very minute." Elias promised to meet both of them later and turned to go inside. His middle still ached, but he knew there was no time to think about it now.

As soon as he saw Elias, Morton Lieberman began complaining. "Where have you been? I was sick with worry. You know I depend on you in the mornings." The little man stretched out his chubby hands and waited to be lifted to his feet. Every morning, Elias dutifully helped Mr. Lieberman off the mattress, but today the ache in his belly made the task very difficult.

Elias bit down on his bottom lip as he pulled upward.

Lieberman didn't notice Elias's pained expression and began snapping his fingers for his jacket. After placing his arms through the sleeves, Lieberman stuck his hand into an inside pocket and pulled out his solid gold pocket watch. For the first time that morning, Morton Lieberman had a smile on his face.

"What a magnificent piece of craftsmanship, and it keeps perfect time. It is now exactly twenty-three minutes before eight o'clock. Oh, I know some people might say it was an extravagance, but I don't regret purchasing this beauty for a second." Carefully he tucked the watch in place and pulled out a handkerchief. He began blowing his nose vigorously. "Oy, it will be a miracle if I make it to Galveston alive," he muttered.

By now, Elias was used to hearing Lieberman grumble all the time. Besides, on this ship everyone complained. Sleeping night after night on lumpy bags of hay upset them all. Elias was very grateful for the scarf his mother had knitted him. At least, his face was protected from the scratchy bedding. He went to pat his prized possession and remembered that Debra was wearing the scarf on her head. His gesture must have made Lieberman think about the scarf as well.

"Do you mean to tell me you went out without a scarf? I don't have the strength to take care of myself, let alone a sick boy."

Quietly, Elias began to explain what had happened with the two Germans. Lieberman became very excited.

"You stay away from them. What would I do if anything happened to you?" The man's right eye began to twitch and immediately Elias was sorry he had mentioned the incident.

"Please, Mr. Lieberman," Elias whispered, "don't get so upset. I'm just fine."

"Well, I'm not! I need to see the doctor, at once!"

Elias was certain that Morton Lieberman was the only Jew on board who still had faith in the ship's doctor. All immigrants, whether Poles, Germans, or Bulgarians, were required to be examined daily. The Jewish passengers quickly realized that the doctor had no interest in their well-being. His only concern was punching a hole in their identification cards. "He inspects the cards, not us," they joked among themselves. Still, everyone visited the infirmary once a day. No one wanted to risk deportation at the Port of Galveston because of an incomplete health record.

"Perhaps after some breakfast you'll feel better. Let's go to the doctor's after we eat." The pain in Elias's belly had suddenly disappeared. In its place were hunger pangs.

Lieberman frowned. "If it were just a matter of food, I'd be the first one in the dining room." Knowing it was futile to argue, Elias resigned himself to waiting at the infirmary on an empty stomach. As they stood in line, Lieberman continued to complain about each ache and annoyance. Once more Elias suggested that a meal might be helpful. The mention of food only enraged Lieberman. Then a stranger tapped him on the shoulder.

"If I were you, sir," he said in Yiddish, "I wouldn't be so quick to trust these doctors. I've heard some real horror stories. They don't bother to diagnose. Everything is cholera to them. If they should quarantine you with the infectious ones, you're a dead man for sure." Lieberman was about to ask a question, but the stranger didn't give him a chance. Waving his inspection card in the air, the passenger declared, "On one ship they buried thirty-two bodies at sea."

Morton Lieberman paled. Without a single word, he stepped out of line and started down the stairway to the dining hall. Elias turned around and grabbed the stranger's hand. He began shaking it with all his might.

"Thank you. Thank you. No one could have given me a nicer birthday present." He knew after breakfast he must return to the clinic to have his card punched, but for now, Elias chased after Lieberman with renewed strength.

The morning prayer service had just concluded in the dining hall, and lines for breakfast were forming rapidly. The Galveston agents had arranged for a kosher kitchen on board the ship. Always fearful that their separate facility would run out of food, the Jewish passengers often shoved and elbowed one another.

Shlomo was waiting near the front of the line when he saw Elias come through the doors. He shouted and waved to his new friend to join him. Elias pulled Lieberman over to meet Shlomo. He was about to introduce everyone when the other people in line started protesting.

"Hey, get out of here!" a man yelled.

"Back of the line. Wait your turn like everyone else," said another.

"The nerve of some people," a woman remarked.

Elias mumbled his apologies as he meekly stepped out of line. But Mr. Lieberman wasn't about to give up a spot so close to the food.

"What kind of human beings are you that you would begrudge a sick man some breakfast?" he whined. "I didn't think I would have the strength to get here, and now you want me to stand in line for hours?"

"You don't look any weaker than the rest of us," remarked the woman with a sleepy toddler in her arms. "If small children can wait, so can you."

"Yeah," the men behind her agreed. Mr. Lieberman felt

someone jab him in the hip. He lost his footing and stumbled out of line. The people around him began to applaud.

Shlomo had just picked up his bowl and was next to be served. To everyone's amazement, he turned to Morton Lieberman.

"Sir, you take my place and I'll keep Elias company in the back."

Morton Lieberman smiled victoriously. He raised his double chins high in the air.

"Thank you," he said pompously.

"Somehow," Elias confided to Shlomo, "he always manages to get his way."

2

Double Portions

PEOPLE WERE CHEERING WILDLY. After fifteen days at sea, the SS *Frankfurt* was sailing into the Baltimore harbor. Elias was screaming with the rest of the crowd.

"Be still!" ordered Lieberman who insisted on grumbling even as he caught his first glimpse of America. "All this commotion is giving me a headache. I'll go deaf from the noise. And why are these fools carrying on so? Most of us have another ten days on this death trap. We're not in Galveston yet."

Elias stopped yelling. Still, his face beamed with excitement.

"Come on, Mr. Lieberman," he teased good-naturedly. "Even you must admit that this is a wonderful day. Look! There's America!" Elias stretched out both arms in the direction of the bustling port. Sailors, fishermen, peddlers, schoolboys, housewives—even a barking dog—scurried about the docks.

Lieberman looked at all the smiling faces around him and his own frown deepened. "How can I be happy?" he muttered under his breath.

"What's that?" asked Elias.

"I've never been a well man, but the problems I've had on this ship! It just doesn't seem fair," whined Lieberman in his most pathetic voice. "And now this business with my eyes. The itching started early this morning. It's such a nuisance. Of course, I'm scared to death to rub them. Everyone knows that's the worst thing you can do."

Elias leaned over to examine Lieberman's eyes. They looked slightly pinkish, but really no redder than his own.

"It's just fatigue, sir. We're all suffering from it."

"It's more than that, I tell you!" The chubby man squeezed his eyes shut and began to jerk his neck from side to side.

Elias didn't want to laugh. He realized that Lieberman was trying to get rid of the itchiness without touching his eyes. But to the fourteen-year-old, it looked as though Lieberman was about to snap his head off his body. Although he was biting down hard on his bottom lip, Elias doubted he would be able to control himself much longer. He brought his large hands up to his mouth and started to giggle. The moment Lieberman opened his eyes, Elias pretended to be clearing his throat.

"You look fine. Really!" said Elias as his hands dropped to his sides. "Besides you're certain to feel better tonight. They're restocking all the supplies this afternoon. They've promised a terrific dinner."

"Well, I would hope so!" snapped Lieberman. "Another day and we would have starved completely. Do you know I almost fainted a few times?"

Elias didn't agree that the situation had ever become that

extreme, but he too was totally disgusted with their meatless meals and meager scraps of bread. After their first week at sea, the Jewish passengers had learned that all their kosher beef and chicken had spoiled. Then, to make matters worse, the kitchen had reported a shortage of flour. In the last six days, steerage passengers had received only a single roll at mealtimes, and often that was either stale or moldy. Elias had gone to bed hungry several times.

But why complain now? he thought to himself as he looked out at his new country. He stepped away from Lieberman so that he could rejoice some more.

As he continued to move backward, he felt his boot brush against someone.

"Excuse me," said Elias to the youngster behind him.

The kick in the shin hadn't bothered the small boy. In fact, the child did not even bother to look up at Elias. He was too busy tugging at the corner of his father's jacket.

"Papa! Papa! I can't see!"

Elias smiled when he saw the father lift the son above his head and anchor him firmly on his shoulders. A small hand popped into the air, and the child started waving.

The little boy reminded Elias of his younger brother, Reuben. The day Elias left, six-year-old Reuben had been sitting on their father's shoulders.

Elias remembered how he had pressed his nose against the cold train window to look out at everyone. He remembered that his parents were holding hands and that with her free arm, his mother had kept pointing to her neck and wiggling her fingers in the air. At the time Elias had understood exactly, because almost every night during those last two weeks Mrs. Cherevnosky had delivered the same lecture.

"I trust that you won't neglect your health, Elias," she had commented each time she had pulled out the red yarn from her sewing bag. "Scarves, hats, and gloves are very important in cold weather. Even on the ship—that sea air is damp. I don't expect to receive any letters about you being sick with pneumonia or frostbite." So that his mother knew he understood, Elias had held the red scarf up to the window and wrapped it around his neck.

Meanwhile little Reuben never stopped waving. Even during those last seconds when he could no longer distinguish faces, Elias remembered watching that tiny arm swinging overhead in the gray, drizzling sky.

Lost in his own thoughts, Elias did not see Shlomo step beside him.

"Welcome to the land of the free and the home of the rich," boomed Zusstovetch, and the excited young man from Kiev gave Elias a hearty slap on the back. Elias jolted forward.

"You scared me," he laughed nervously. He took a moment to catch his breath. "You really shouldn't sneak up on a person like that."

"I tried to get your attention, but you've been standing here in some sort of trance. What's so special about that kid, anyway?" Shlomo pointed up at the boy on his father's shoulders.

Elias shrugged. "Nothing really. He just reminded me of Reuben."

Shlomo nodded that he understood. In the last ten days, Elias and he had become good friends on the ship, and Shlomo had heard a lot about the Cherevnoskys from Gomel.

"Don't start getting homesick on me now. Before you know it, the day will come when you'll be greeting your folks in Galveston. By then, you'll be a full-fledged American, and I bet when you see Reuben, he'll be waving just like that little one." Shlomo glanced up at the child. The boy must have heard him for he looked down at the exact same moment. Zusstovetch winked at the lad and without any hesitation, the youngster winked back at Shlomo. All three burst out laughing, but the laughter stopped as soon as Elias saw Lieberman signal him for help.

"Where have you been? I turn around and you've disappeared." Elias tried to explain, but Lieberman just shook his head in disgust.

"How many times must I repeat myself? You know I need assistance. And don't think I didn't see you laughing with Shlomo over there. You two are always wandering off somewhere. Just remember who's paying your way, young man. I chose you because I thought you were responsible."

"But—"

"No buts! Now come," ordered Lieberman. "Let's get to the clinic before some of those animals start pushing and shoving with their cards."

That day Elias felt envious of anyone whose destination was Baltimore. He and Shlomo were especially disappointed that all immigrants continuing to Galveston were required to stay on board while the ship was docked in the harbor. In the afternoon while Lieberman napped and Debra crocheted with the other ladies, Shlomo and Elias sat on deck and watched the crew carry on fresh supplies. Their mouths watered when they saw the crate of kosher meats, but it was the rumor about the bread which excited them most. Supposedly, everyone would be getting double portions of dinner rolls for the remainder of the trip.

"You see," exclaimed Shlomo. "This is America. Life is better already. You can almost smell prosperity in the air."

Elias closed his eyes and inhaled. "How right you are," he agreed. All the time he was trying to remember the aroma of freshly baked bread. "Of course," he added in a voice mimicking Lieberman's, "after all we've been through, two rolls at dinner is the least they can do."

"True," agreed Shlomo. "For Bremen alone we should get triple portions of everything!"

When he heard the name "Bremen," Elias shuddered. Like all the other passengers, Lieberman and he had boarded the SS *Frankfurt* in Bremen, Germany.

"Did you happen to stay at the Stadt Warshaw?" he asked Shlomo.

"Only for one night." All of a sudden, Shlomo had a mischievous grin on his face.

"What's so funny?" asked Elias.

"I can just imagine your Uncle Morton's face when he saw that pigsty. I see how crazy he gets about germs. To be honest, I expected to catch something myself."

"You don't know the half of it. We had to sleep there for a week and what happened that first day was really embarrassing." Elias hesitated.

"Well?" asked Shlomo.

"I don't know if I should talk about it. It makes me so angry when I think about it."

Shlomo rubbed his palms together. "Ooh! Those are the best stories. Come on, Elias."

"Okay, but don't mention it to anyone else. To start with, neither of us could believe we were at the right address." As Elias began the story, he slipped into Lieberman's whiny tone.

"'This must be a mistake. The Galveston recruiter couldn't have made such arrangements for us. After all, I paid good money for these fares. This week in Germany is costing me a fortune and just so I can wait for a boat!'" Elias paused. He was still unsure he should tell the rest.

"Go on. Go on," Shlomo coaxed. "I love the way you tell a story."

"Well, while he complained about money, I stood there holding my nose. The smell in that place was awful. And the flies were everywhere. But to be honest, Uncle Morton remained fairly calm—that is until he saw the sleeping accommodations. Then he demanded to speak to the manager." Recalling every gesture, Elias proceeded to reenact the scene in Bremen.

"'Excuse me, I believe the gentleman in Gomel who made the arrangements for my nephew and me neglected to mention that we require privacy when we sleep. Unfortunately, I'm not a well man, and a good night's rest for me is crucial. I won't be able to sleep in a room with all those people. There must be forty at least. Besides, I suspect there's not even a mattress for everyone. It's most unsanitary, you know.'"

"'So what do you want me to do about it,'" grunted the manager.

Lieberman leaned forward and whispered, "'I'm sure I could make it worth your while if you could find us a decent room, perhaps in another lodging house—with a kosher kitchen, of course.'"

The manager grinned. "'Sure I can help you,'" and he stuck out his big sweaty palm in front of Lieberman's face. The Hebrew teacher hesitated for just a moment. Then he gave the German a handful of coins.

"'Come back in the morning,'" said the manager as he dropped the money in his pocket.

"'But what about tonight? We refuse to sleep in such filth.'"

The clerk began to snicker. "'You fool. The local police assign you people to these lodging houses. You can't pick and choose.'"

"'But you took my money!'"

"'What money? I don't see any money,'" and the German walked away jingling the change in his pocket.

"I can still hear that money rattling in his pants," Elias said to Shlomo. His face had become more and more flushed as he remembered the scene in Bremen. "He made such fools of us. But the worst part was that we were trapped there for a week, and everyday we had to face that man's obnoxious grin."

"So what? As I see it, you still got the last laugh. After all, we're the ones on our way to Galveston. Long after you've made a fortune in America, that bum will still be swatting flies in a smelly hole."

Elias's face lit up with a big smile. "I hadn't quite thought of it that way. Oh, I hope you're right about a fortune," he sighed.

"Of course I am!" cried out Shlomo. "Why I can tell that things are different already."

That night, Elias had to agree with his friend. Unlike other evenings, no one pushed in line. The delicious aroma of chicken roasting and the promise of freshly baked rolls had put everyone in a festive mood.

Elias's eyes opened wide as he watched the servers generously spoon out the white rice and candied carrots. To his delight, the rumor had been correct. He received two plump rolls on the side of his platter.

Even Morton Lieberman looked content. As Elias went to sit down, Mr. Lieberman waved him away, motioning for Elias to sit down at the next table. "Tonight, eat with your friends. Enjoy yourself."

"Really?"

Lieberman nodded and Elias hurried to an empty seat next to Shlomo. Together, the two boys and Debra recited the blessing over the bread. Elias pronounced an emphatic "Amen" and took a big chunk out of the roll.

No sooner had he swallowed the first bite, than he heard someone call out to him. "Elias Cherevnosky get over here. Your Uncle has fainted."

Elias pushed back his chair and ran to Lieberman's side. He lifted the man's chin off the plate and gently patted the pudgy cheeks. Bits of rice fell to the table. After a few seconds, Morton Lieberman opened his eyes.

"What happened?" he asked groggily.

"You fainted," answered Elias. "I guess you meant it today when you said you were starving."

Lieberman looked around as if he didn't know where he was. Others near him didn't seem surprised.

"Just a case of light-headedness," said the woman across from him. Her mouth was full of bread. "It's a miracle more of us haven't fainted." Everyone echoed her sentiments and encouraged Lieberman to begin eating. But for some reason, the man couldn't stand to look at the food. Finally, Elias grabbed a roll from Lieberman's platter.

"Here. At least have this."

The Hebrew teacher's eyes opened wide and he shook his head furiously. "The ro-ro-roll!" he stuttered. He broke into a sweat; his body was trembling.

Elias examined the roll. It looked fine. He tore it apart. The dough was still warm. Elias couldn't resist and bit off a chunk.

"It's delicious."

Lieberman shook his head adamantly and pointed to the second piece of bread. Elias noticed it had a small crack on top. He picked it up but dropped it like a hot potato when he saw the little black head sticking out from the crust. It fell in front of the very woman who had been coaxing Lieberman to eat. She glanced down and let out a frightened scream.

"Is that a cockroach in the bread?" Her shrill cry brought a sudden hush to the dining room. In a matter of minutes everyone was checking the food for bugs. One other cockroach was found in Debra's roll. Seconds later, Elias and Shlomo were inside the kitchen.

"What are you doing in here?" yelled the portly cook when he saw the boys walking toward him. Elias and Shlomo recognized Fritz at once. All the passengers knew him. The sailors often joked that the only thing bigger than Fritz's belly was the cook's hot temper.

"No one comes into my kitchen uninvited. You Jews don't have to worry. Everything is kosher. Now out! Out! Out!" His puffy cheeks grew redder with each shriek and his eyes seemed to be popping out of his head.

"Look! We found cockroaches in your food." Shlomo yelled back at him. Then he threw the rolls at the cook. They landed in a bowl on the work table. "Impossible!" insisted Fritz. With a large wooden ladle, he scooped up the pieces of bread. He saw the baked cockroaches buried in the dough and winced.

"It's a mistake," he repeated over and over again. "No one would do that on purpose. I'll give you two more rolls. Now leave me alone."

Suddenly, someone started cackling. The boys turned their attention to a sailor in the corner of the kitchen. He was leaning forward with his elbows planted firmly on the seat of a stool. In one hand, he held a stein of beer. In the other, he was waving a meaty chicken leg. Before he could even see the man's face, Elias recognized the laugh.

"Fritzi," bellowed the intoxicated sailor, "you did a good thing. These people must get used to eating bugs. In America, that's all they feed Jews."

"You're drunk," shouted Shlomo.

"True. True. But at least, I'm not a fool traveling halfway around the world for an opportunity that doesn't exist."

"What do you know?" Elias sneered.

"Yeah!" mocked Shlomo. "Why, you're lucky if they let you mop the floors."

With the beer still in one hand and the chicken leg in the other, the sailor staggered toward the boys. He was looking straight at Shlomo.

"Watch him," whispered Elias. "That's the one who socked me in the belly."

The drunk belched in Shlomo's face. Then he turned to Elias. "Tell your friend that in a few months, he'll be begging for a job like mine. He'll be begging for any job. But nobody is gonna want him. And do you know why? Because he's a dirty—" As the sailor started to pronounce "Jew," his massive right arm flung out toward Elias. But this time, Elias was ready. He ducked to the side and swung his leg in front of the moving sailor. The German tumbled forward. His clay mug shattered into bits and pieces. Ale splattered all over the floor and the greasy chicken bone slid across the room.

"Look what you've done!" shrieked Fritz. "Get up you lazy good-for-nothing and clean up this mess. How dare you start brawling in my kitchen!" The cook grabbed a heavy broom and started toward the sailor. But the furious cook took no precautions as he stormed across the wet surface. Suddenly, one of his chunky legs flew up into the air. A second later, Fritz was on his back and cursing wildly.

Elias tapped Shlomo on the shoulder and pointed to the door. As soon as they were out of the kitchen, the boys broke into a fit of laughter. When Lieberman saw them, he leaped to his feet.

"So? What happened?"

Elias first regained his composure. "For this night alone," he exclaimed, "the whole ordeal has been worth it." Then together Shlomo and Elias described the scene in the kitchen.

All the Jewish passengers loved the story. Morton Lieberman was especially proud to be the man who had triggered the event. That night he boasted to everyone that "thanks to him the Germans had been taught a good lesson."

It was after midnight when Elias finally plopped down on his bed. But he wasn't tired and the scratchy hay was even more annoying than usual. He lay awake with his eyes open and started to think about the sailor. He was proud of himself for having dodged the bully, but for some reason the drunk's ugly remarks began to haunt Elias.

"What will I do if I can't find work?" wondered Elias. "What if they haven't told us the truth? Could Mama have been right all along?"

"Why must it be Galveston?" Dena Cherevnosky had wanted to know when she first heard about the Galveston Movement. "Why not New York or Philadelphia? That's where all the Russian Jews have settled."

Elias recalled watching the Jewish Emigration Society agent heave a particularly long and exasperated sigh.

"Oy. I hear that comment at least once a day, madam. Unfortunately, people don't want to face facts. You see, Mrs. Cherevnosky, although it is true that America is a land of opportunity, the Eastern Seaboard is terribly overcrowded. Especially New York. Our program is designed to place the new immigrant where good-paying jobs are readily available. In fact, right now we have agents lining up work all over the country."

Still, Dena had some reservations and privately expressed her doubts to Jacob. "If there's so much money to be made, why haven't the Jews in America flocked to these cities? After all, can everyone in New York be a millionaire already?"

Secretly, Mr. Cherevnosky shared some of his wife's skepticism, but he refused to say or do anything which would jeopardize Elias's one opportunity to get out of Russia.

For most of his adult life, Jacob Cherevnosky had wanted to take his family to New York. But though he tried hard the tailor had never been able to save enough money to leave Gomel. As the years passed, his plan began to sound more and more impossible. That is, until the spring of 1907, when Morton Lieberman decided to sign up for the Galveston Movement.

"At least," Jacob told his friends proudly, "my Elias will have his chance. If he works very hard, with his salary and the little I can save we all can go to America soon."

"Oh, Papa," moaned Elias, lying on his scratchy mattress, "I hope I don't disappoint you."

For the next several days, Elias walked around the ship, brooding. Whenever Shlomo asked him what was the matter, young Cherevnosky insisted there was nothing wrong. Finally, by the fifth day, Shlomo remarked, "I never noticed it before, but I'm beginning to see a real resemblance between you and Uncle Morton. I suppose it's the way you both are always so cheerful, lately."

"Shh," whispered Debra, who was standing between the boys. But even she couldn't suppress a tiny giggle.

"I'm sorry I haven't been very good company. It's just that I have a lot on my mind."

"But why be worried now?" asked Shlomo. "For us, the worst is over!"

"Perhaps for you and Debra. After all, you have someone waiting in Kansas City, but I don't even know where I'm going."

"So?"

"So, there may not be enough work. I might not make enough money for my parents and brother to join me. What if I never see them again?"

"Well!" huffed Shlomo in a sarcastic voice. "With an attitude like that, you might as well stay on this wonderful boat and sail back to our paradise in Russia."

Debra's cheeks were suddenly bright red. This time her brother's sarcasm had not amused her. "How dare you joke about such a matter?" she cried. "What do you mean sail back? Back to what? Poverty? Pogroms? They trampled on us with their horses and burned down our houses. They killed and maimed and no one uttered a sound. Oh, no! There is no going back!"

Her tone startled them both into a stunned silence. Elias lowered his head in shame. Hadn't his commitment always been irreversible? How could he have forgotten so soon? His family was trapped without his help. There was no alternative but to succeed.

3

Galveston

AS THEY RACED down the gangway at the Port of Galveston, the children squealed with delight. The adults walked more slowly. Many had tears falling down their tired faces. Some stepped off the ship and dropped to their knees to kiss the land beneath them.

Debra Resnick was like a little girl, darting in and out between the other passengers. Yussell Resnick studied the faces in the crowd, but he couldn't find his wife.

"I'm here, Yussell. Yussell, I'm here," Debra shouted.

The man turned his head and saw his wife running with opened arms. In the next moment, they were wrapped in each other's embrace.

Still on deck, Elias watched the reunion. A few seconds later, he saw Shlomo fling his arms around the couple.

Elias turned to Morton Lieberman, who was seated beside him. He had refused to exit until the crowd had dispersed.

"People get too excited," he had grumbled to Elias. "I didn't come all this way to be trampled in a stampede. We'll wait until almost everyone is off the ship."

Elias sat there tapping his foot. He could hear his heart pounding inside of him. Every few minutes he looked over at Lieberman, but the man showed no sign of budging. When the ship looked almost deserted, Elias stood up.

"Well? Can we go?" he pleaded.

Without murmuring a sound, Lieberman rose to dust off the sleeves of his rumpled overcoat. Then he jutted his double chins up toward the clouds and raised his elbow. Elias quickly picked up his bag and looped his free arm through Lieberman's. Together they began a slow, dignified walk off the ship.

They followed the crowd into the immigration building. Doctors, government officials, and Galveston agents were waiting inside. Elias and Lieberman were still at the back of the line when Shlomo ran over.

"Look! It's official. My American name is Sam. Sam Zussman." Shlomo held up his papers. Elias grabbed them and inspected the foreign words.

"Do they ask a lot of questions?"

"Not too many. They seem more interested in your health. If you're an able body, they're happy to admit you."

Mr. Lieberman began jerking his head.

"Please, Mr. Lieberman," whispered Elias. "Don't get nervous. Your eyes look no worse than anyone else's."

"That's true, sir," chimed in Shlomo. "If you don't complain, they won't suspect a thing."

"No one knows how I suffer," muttered Lieberman.

Elias pretended not to hear the remark and turned to Shlomo. "Where's Debra?"

"I wanted to give her and Yussell some time alone," he answered with a wink. Then he added, "They have wagons waiting for us. We go to the headquarters for the Jewish Immigrants' Information Bureau here in Galveston. Yussell says we'll get to take a warm bath and have a good kosher meal there.

Morton Lieberman grunted. "Sure. Now, they try to make up for the last twenty-five days." He jerked his head several times.

Again, Elias ignored the Hebrew school teacher. Instead, he asked Shlomo, "Do we stay in Galveston tonight?"

"I don't know what the plan is for everyone. Yussell said that Kansas City people leave right after the meal. Aren't you eager to find out where they're sending you, Elias? It's all so exciting, isn't it?"

For Shlomo's sake Elias tried to look enthusiastic, but really, he was scared more than anything. His palms were clammy. He took a couple of deep breaths to try to relax.

The line moved quickly. One of the agents recognized Shlomo in the back and motioned for him to follow those who were ready to board the first wagon. Shlomo insisted that he had to wait with Elias, but the inspector was just as persistent and ordered him to stay with his group.

"Save us two seats at your dinner table," Elias called out as Shlomo stepped outside.

A few moments later, Elias and Mr. Lieberman were standing in front of the Port Marine Surgeon. The doctor examined Elias first.

"He's fine," said the doctor, and Elias was sent over to the immigration inspector's desk where the boy was asked to present his papers.

"Oh, these names! These names!" groaned the officer as he read the top line of Elias's form. "Elias Che-Che-re-no-"

"Elias Cherevnosky," the boy said easily.

"Too long!" snapped the tired officer. He closed his eyes and Elias waited. A few seconds later, the officer exclaimed, "Elias Cherry!" and wrote the name in large print at the top of the document. Elias watched how the man carefully formed each letter, but the English alphabet made no sense to him. When the officer finished writing he looked up and saw Elias's troubled expression. Again he repeated, "Cherry. Elias Cherry."

"Cherry. Elias Cherry," the boy mimicked. Then Elias turned around to see whether Lieberman had completed the physical examination. Two Galveston agents were standing by the doctor. Both were speaking in Yiddish and English.

"What's the problem, Uncle?"

"Who are you?" demanded one of the agents.

"Elias Cherevnosky. From Gomel."

"And this is your Uncle?"

"Of course," lied Elias.

"How old are you?" the second agent said.

"Seventeen." Elias stood up as straight as he could.

The agent turned to the doctor. "But he's all right?" he asked, pointing to Elias. The doctor motioned for the boy to step closer so he could re-examine his eyes. "Looks perfect. It's just the uncle."

"Please," Elias said in Yiddish. "What's the problem?" Before anyone could say a word, Morton Lieberman began ranting and raving.

"It's just what I've been telling everyone," he screamed. "But you all insisted it was only fatigue. Well, now," he gloated, "I have the confirmation of a learned physician from the United States of America. And to think no one believed me!"

"Uncle, what are you talking about?"

"I have traucoma—an eye infection. This itching has not been a figment of my imagination—although I know a few people who would have liked me to believe this was the case."

Elias didn't know how to react. Lieberman sounded so pleased—almost victorious that he had proven everyone wrong. "How long will my uncle be quarantined?" he asked.

"He'll have to return to Bremen," the agent said flatly. "Traucoma means an automatic deportation. When he's cured, you can both return."

"Oy," moaned Lieberman, who no longer was sounding so smug. "Such things only happen to me. Well, I've been telling people I'm an unlucky, sick man for years. What can I do?"

"Don't worry, sir. These cases can clear up in a few weeks," the doctor assured him.

"Well, if I'm sick, I'm sick. Come on, Elias."

Elias didn't budge.

"What are you waiting for?" said Lieberman. "Pick up the bags."

"No. I want to stay."

Lieberman rolled his eyes and grunted. "You're only a child. You can't do such a thing."

"Wait a minute. The lad says he's seventeen," interrupted one of the agents. "He's perfectly capable of taking care of himself."

"This is none of your affair," Lieberman shouted back at him. Then he realized he had no say in the matter. After all, it would be very unwise to admit they had lied. The agent in Gomel had been quite specific. The Galveston Movement had no interest in recruiting Hebrew school teachers, and Lieberman certainly didn't want to forfeit his chance to return in a month or two. In a much calmer voice he said, "I apologize for the outburst. I'm sure you can understand my disappointment and frustration. If you please, I would like to speak to my nephew in private."

The doctor and agents turned their attention to the last few passengers waiting in line. Lieberman took Elias by the elbow and pulled him to a corner of the room.

"You know very well I can't return without you. What will your father say?"

"He'll probably never find out. I suspect by the time you arrive in Bremen, you'll be fine and will come back on the next ship. Besides, I know my father would want me to stay. I've got to start earning money, Mr. Lieberman. Anyway, do you really want to pay for my fare all over again?"

The last argument convinced the Hebrew teacher, but he didn't want to appear too eager about the decision. "I'm not a well person," he whined. "I can't fight with you. Just remember, you're deserting a very sick man. I hope I survive the journey back and here again."

Elias hesitated. Had he underestimated the seriousness of Lieberman's condition all along? While he stood there debating what he should do, Lieberman interpreted the boy's silence as a sign of defiance. He walked away in a huff. Elias was about to run after him when he felt a tapping on his shoulder.

"So what have you decided?" asked the agent. "The last group is ready to board the wagon."

Elias looked over at the stocky little man jerking his head from side to side. He looks so pathetic, the boy thought to himself.

"Tell me," Elias asked the agent, "where do they plan to send me?"

"Sorry, that information is at headquarters. But don't worry, we'll get word to your uncle. You should only be separated two or three months."

Elias walked over to Lieberman. "They'll let you know where I'll be. And of course I'll write my parents. Maybe you'll all come back together."

Boy!" yelled the agent from the doorway. "If you're riding with us, let's go."

Elias grabbed Lieberman's hand. "Thank you for bringing me. I will always be in your debt." Lieberman pulled away. Slowly Elias turned toward the door.

"Here," Lieberman called out. "Take this."

Elias stopped and looked down at the man's open palm. "But sir, that's your gold pocket watch!"

"I'm not giving it to you," snapped Lieberman. "But in case of an emergency, it should bring you a decent price. Mind you, it's just a loan."

Elias smiled as he slipped the watch into his coat pocket. Suddenly, he felt Lieberman's arms around him. "You're such a good boy," whispered the man. "Take care of yourself." Then he turned away from Elias.

"Come on!" barked the agent. As Elias ran out the door, Lieberman stood on his tiptoes and looked out at the wagon with envy. Riding away, Elias kept wondering if he were doing the right thing. Making his way alone was much more than he had ever bargained for. As he tried to imagine the adventure ahead, he shivered with excitement.

The Bureau was only a half-mile away. After their miserable sailing accommodations, the Bureau, with its bright lighting and proper ventilation, was a welcome sight. The shelter provided washrooms, showers, baths, cots, a kosher kitchen, dining tables, and chairs. As one of the last to bathe, Elias enjoyed the luxury of taking his time. Afterwards, he joined Debra and Shlomo.

"There you are! We thought you drowned in there," laughed Shlomo.

Debra turned to her husband. "Yussell, this is our friend, Elias Cherevnosky."

Yussell stood up and offered his hand. Although he was a slight man, his grip was powerful. "I'm happy to meet you. My wife and brother-in-law have had many kind words for the famous Elias Cherevnosky from Gomel."

Elias blushed. "Thank you. But, it's 'Cherry' now," the boy added with a self-conscious giggle.

"So you got an American name, too!" said Shlomo. "Good for you!"

"Where's your uncle?" asked Debra.

"There was a problem at the immigration office."

Debra's eyes flashed wide open. "What happened?"

Elias shifted his weight from one foot to the other. He still wasn't certain he had made the right decision and felt uncomfortable talking about it. "You know how he complained about his eyes? The doctor says he has traucoma. They're sending him back."

"For good?" asked Shlomo.

"No, no. Just until the eye infection clears up. But we decided it was silly for me to go back and forth with him."

"Definitely," agreed Yussell. "It's better that you start earning some money. There's a lot of opportunity, but if you don't take advantage, someone else will. You never know if there will be a second chance." Yussell's comments made Elias feel a little easier about the unfortunate circumstance and he pulled up a chair.

During the meal, Rabbi Henry Cohen and Mr. Morris Waldman, two highly respected leaders of the Movement and the men in charge of the Bureau in Galveston, greeted everyone in Yiddish. Their remarks were full of praise and encouragement. Afterward, the immigrants stood up and applauded.

As they were sitting down again, Yussell told Shlomo and Elias, "When I arrived with the first group on July first, none of us could believe it. The Mayor himself made a special trip down here to meet us. We were thrilled to think such an important man would come to shake our hands. These big, grown men had tears in their eyes."

"Do you suppose he's coming today?" asked Shlomo.

"I don't know," laughed Yussell, "but don't worry, Shlomo. Kansas City has its share of officials. You'll have your chance, one day."

"I plan to," answered Shlomo with a big grin. "I'm an American now! Who knows? Maybe I'll be mayor one day."

Yussell elbowed Elias. "And I guess Mr. Cherry over here plans to be governor."

"Why not?" Elias replied boldly. "Of course for right now, I just want to know where I'll be living."

Debra leaned over and whispered in Yussell's ear. "Can't Elias come with us? He's all alone. It doesn't seem right."

Yussell shook his head and whispered back to Debra, "It's not up to us. They've already placed him. He's got to go where there's a job."

They were just serving dessert when one of the agents asked for everyone's attention. "Please, when you're finished, line up at the desk for your job assignments." Elias was the first one on his feet.

"But, Elias, you didn't eat your piece of apple pie," said Shlomo.

"You can have it." He slid the plate toward Shlomo and ran to be first in line. When Elias identified himself, the agent scanned the list of names.

"Here we go. Elias Cherevnosky sailing with Morton Lieberman. Tailors from Gomel."

"I'm afraid my uncle has been deported."

"Oh, so he's the unlucky fellow. Yeah, I heard something about it."

"They said he has traucoma. But he's coming back."

The agent frowned. "Mmm. This could pose a problem."

Elias's palms were sweating. "Why? The doctor didn't seem concerned. He said Uncle Morton will be back as soon as his eyes clear up."

"Of course. But in the meantime, the job in Wichita requires an experienced tailor. They were only accepting an apprentice because you're the tailor's nephew."

"But Morton Lieberman is not—" Elias caught himself before completing the sentence. He suddenly realized that Lieberman had lied about his profession too.

"What's that?" asked the agent, who at the same time was motioning to another agent for assistance.

"I was, uh, wondering what happens now?"

"I don't know. Maybe you should return with your uncle."

"Please. I've got to stay. My family is still waiting in Gomel. They all want to come to America. They're depending on me to earn some money."

"What's the problem, here? You're holding up the line." Elias turned around and saw another agent behind him.

"We don't have a slot for this one," the first agent shrugged.

"Then put him with the Tennessee group. He looks like a strong one. Memphis always needs more laborers."

Before Elias could protest, the second supervisor walked away to help someone else.

"I don't understand. I expected to be working in a tailor's shop," he mumbled before giving up his place in line.

"It won't be forever, son. Besides, something is better than nothing."

"But you guarantee—"

"We guarantee a job. The rest is up to you. Tonight you sleep here. Your group leaves first thing in the morning." Elias returned to the table.

"So? What did they say?" Shlomo asked with a mouthful of pie.

"I'm off to Memphis."

"That's Tennessee," said Yussell.

"I still don't see why Elias can't come with us," said Debra.

Elias shrugged. "It's not my first choice, either. They've assigned me as a laborer."

Shlomo's jaw dropped. "A common laborer. Don't they know you're an expert tailor?"

I tried to tell them."

"That's too bad," said Yussell. "As a tailor, you would earn more money."

"Really?" asked Elias.

"Sure. For instance," Yussell explained, "I'm a trained carpenter. In Kiev, cabinets were my specialty. When I arrived I began at a salary of ten dollars a week, more than two times what I ever earned in Russia. And yesterday, I was just raised two more dollars."

"Do you mean I'm actually going to earn twelve dollars every week!" gasped Shlomo.

"No!" the brother-in-law answered flatly. "You'll begin lower, but still the salaries are decent. A friend of mine recently heard about a tailor's apprentice who was once hired by Birenbaum's in Kansas City. That's a big store there. Anyway, he swore that the kid started out at eight dollars a week plus free room and board. Not bad, when you don't have to pay for rent or food. Of course, even the people who have no skills can still make five or six dollars a week. So don't feel too bad," he said looking up at Elias.

Elias made a face. "You sound just like the agent."

"Don't fool yourself, Cherevnosky. Even in America, people are poor. If you want a roof over your head and food in your belly, you can't be particular."

By dusk everyone but the five men selected for Memphis were gone. The Kansas City group had been the first to leave. Even as she was riding away, Debra called out to Elias, "Remember, you're always welcome in our home."

In the evening, the men were treated to another delicious kosher meal. Afterward, the agents brought out cots, blankets, and pillows for their overnight guests. Exhausted from all the excitement of the day, the other four fell asleep easily. Only Elias was wide awake. With nothing to do and no one to talk to, he walked around the room aimlessly. One of the agents suggested he look through a basket of Yiddish newspapers.

"You must be overtired," said the officer. "Lie on your cot and read. You'll fall asleep quickly enough."

At first he wasn't too interested in a seven-week-old newspaper dated September 29, and casually flipped through the pages. Starting to yawn from boredom, Elias was just about to toss the paper on the floor when he spotted a headline near the bottom of the back page:

MOVEMENT IMPORTING IMMIGRANTS FOR SLAVERY

Elias sat up straight. The article was about the Galveston Movement.

The newspaper contended that the safety of all Jewish immigrants was in jeopardy because of the peculiar "convict-lease" system established in the South. In order for laborers to secure work in states like Louisiana and Tennessee, they were obligated to sign a contract with their bosses. Some of the immigrants who had recently arrived through the Port of Galveston found that they had agreed to be members of work gangs, toiling for meager amounts of food and water only. To run away was a punishable offense, and if convicted, the immigrant was automatically sentenced to a chain gang. "They still believe in slavery!" Elias whispered under his breath. He had read about the Civil War to free the black people in America. He never imagined that Russian Jews were the next victims.

Elias reread the article several times. Nervously, he kept pulling on a loose thread in his red scarf. When he looked down, he realized he had pulled apart some of his mother's beautiful handiwork. Immediately, he tried to repair the damage, but without a needle, his efforts were in vain. As he struggled with the strand of wool he thought about the morning he had given Debra the scarf. Oh, if only he had been assigned to Kansas City.!

Maybe, I should go there anyway, he thought to himself. Suddenly, he remembered something Yussell had told him and started to plot out his strategy. He looked across the room and noticed the two men sorting papers by the filing cabinet. He recognized one of them as the agent who had assigned him to Memphis.

Elias sat on his cot for several minutes and rehearsed what he planned to tell them. Finally, he took a deep breath and walked over to the cabinet. At first he stood there unnoticed. Then the agent who had helped the boy earlier stopped working.

"Can we do something for you?" he asked.

"I've changed my mind," announced Elias.

The other gentleman slammed shut the cabinet drawer. "What do you mean? You want to return to Russia?" he asked in an incredulous tone.

"Oh, no," Elias assured him. "I want to go to Kansas City with my friends."

The agents smiled at one another. "I'm afraid you greenhorns really believe the nonsense about our streets being paved with gold," said one. "I'm sorry to disillusion you, but it's just not so. I don't recommend going anywhere without a job. Believe me, Memphis is a good city. They need strong workers."

Elias could feel little beads of perspiration forming on his forehead and above his upper lip, but he didn't hesitate for a second.

"It just so happens that if I want work at Birenbaum's with pay plus room and board, the job is mine."

"Why didn't you mention this earlier when I was processing your papers?"

Elias looked the agent straight in the eye. "When Yussell Resnick came to pick up his family, he told me about the job. I wanted to go, but I didn't think you would permit me."

The agent's tone softened. "We may not have streets of gold, my friend, but in America, men are free to live where they choose. Of course, getting you there may be a problem."

He turned to the other agent. "Marvin, who's going to Kansas City next?"

The man had a grin on his face. "It just so happens, I have a meeting with Jacob Billikopf next week. The boy can take the train with me." He turned to Elias and explained, "Mr. Billikopf is our chief officer in Kansas City. He'll help you get settled."

Elias grabbed the man's hand and shook it with terrific enthusiasm. Then he turned and grabbed the other agent's hand. "Thank you," he repeated over and over again.

When Elias returned to his cot, the agents started whispering about the young tailor from Gomel. "So? What do you imagine is the real story? Do you think there is a job waiting for him in K.C.?"

The other shrugged. "How else would he know the name Birenbaum? Anyway, it makes sense. This afternoon in all the excitement, he probably felt like a big shot and wanted to go out on his own. Tonight, with his friends gone, he's lonely. The kid's got a typical case of nerves. Can you blame him?"

From his cot, Elias noticed the agents looking in his direction. He had already stuck the Yiddish newspaper under his blanket. Somehow, he would make sure the others read the article, but he certainly didn't want to call any more attention to himself.

After a hearty breakfast of eggs and toast the next morning, the men began lining up to board the wagon. As the last man was ready to exit, Elias handed him the newspaper.

"Be sure to read the article at the bottom of the back page. I saw it last night. It's about Tennessee. The others must read it, too. It's something you need to know about their laws."

The man shoved the paper in his pocket. "Aren't you coming?"

"No, I've decided to join my friend Shlomo in Kansas City."

The man stretched out his big hand to Elias. "Good luck."

"To you too. And just make sure you and the others read the paper."

"Of course." Elias watched the man pat his pocket as he walked out the door.

4

Mr. Scott

IT WAS ONLY his second morning in Galveston when Elias suddenly felt someone shaking him out of a deep sleep. Slowly, he raised his left eyelid and squinted upward. At first he didn't recognize the blurry image standing by his cot.

"My plans have changed," a voice announced in Yiddish. Elias's eyes flashed wide open and he realized that the face staring down at him belonged to the agent who had promised to take him to Kansas City.

"Wh-what?" he stammered.

The man shrugged. "Got to go to New York, tonight."

"But what about Kansas City? You're not making me go to Memphis, are you?" Elias got up out of his cot and stood shivering in his long underwear.

"Memphis? I thought you said you had a job lined up at Birenbaum's."

"Of course. That's why I must go to Kansas City!" He

blurted out the demand with such force that even Elias was shocked by his own brazenness.

"Hey, son, don't get so excited. I took care of everything. As soon as I learned about my change in plans, I wired Abe Birenbaum to meet you at the station in K.C. tomorrow. He's worked with us before. I don't imagine there should be any problems. But you'd better get hold of that hot temper of yours. Now, get going."

Before leaving the bureau, Elias gulped down a few spoonfuls of oatmeal. He kept thinking, What am I doing? What's going to happen when I get to Kansas City?

As they pulled up to the train station, the conductor was calling, "All aboard!" The agent shoved a train ticket, a few dollars, and a piece of scrap paper into Elias's sweating palm. "I'm sure there won't be any problems, but just in case, there's Birenbaum's address."

Everything happened so quickly. It wasn't until he actually sat down and felt the wheels moving under him that Elias realized he was on his own—no parents, no Galveston agents, no German sailors, and most important, no Morton Lieberman to nag him. From now on, I make all the decisions, he thought. It seemed like a fine idea until he couldn't figure out where to put his bag.

"Tickets! Tickets, please!" the conductor was calling. The words made no sense, but Elias watched a man in a crisp black uniform proceed down the aisle and collect tiny stubs of paper. Elias's fingers trembled as he held out his ticket. Seconds later he was wearing a triumphant grin. Not only had the conductor punched his ticket and placed his bag in the rack above, but the gentleman had even tipped his hat.

"Maybe it's not so obvious I'm an immigrant," thought Elias. He glanced down at his clenched fist, still clinging to the money and the scrap of paper with Birenbaum's address. He relaxed his grip and started to examine the strange currency. He wasn't aware that someone was watching him.

"If you're smart, you'll put your money in your pocket," a voice called over to him.

Elias didn't know that he was the one being spoken to, but he still looked up. The man seated across from him was pointing at the loose dollar bills.

"You're going to lose that, or even worse, some thief will snatch it away from you."

The man's pointing made him very nervous, and Elias shoved everything into his coat pocket. The stranger nodded in approval. Elias smiled back at him.

"So? You on your way to Kansas City for pleasure or business?" asked the stranger who sat there tapping on a big black suitcase.

"Kansas City, Kansas City," Elias replied while nodding his head with enthusiasm.

The man slapped his knee. "How 'bout that. I think I got one right off the boat. Should have known. Coming in through Galveston and everything." The man continued to babble good-naturedly; he seemed quite content to carry on a conversation all by himself. The bald-headed stranger had a bushy silver mustache, and he was very animated when he spoke. Elias enjoyed watching him.

"Ah, Kansas City! Good people. Hard-working people. Fine town. Fine town, indeed. One of the favorites in my territory. Oh, did I mention? I'm a salesman. Scott's the name. Archibald T. Scott."

Without missing a beat, the man snapped open his black suitcase. Elias looked more confused than ever, but the man kept talking.

"Yup. I sell collars for your shirts and garters for your hose. Some might say a funny combination, but I just see it as basic essentials for any well-dressed gentleman. Of course the collars are an easier sell than these contraptions." The salesman picked up a handful of stocking garters and dangled them in front of Elias.

"Don't look so baffled, young feller. These are for your socks. I'd pull up my trousers and show you, but I don't think the ladies across the way would approve." He turned toward two grim-looking women on the other side of the aisle and winked. They turned their heads with a huff, and the salesman started laughing. Elias began squirming in his seat.

"Oh, don't get in a tizzy, young feller. Those two old crows have been eavesdropping on us since we said our howdy-do's. And they've been eyein' you over ever since you plopped down in that seat. I get a real kick out of all these people who put on such airs. As if their families weren't foreigners, once. Ha! In America, everyone comes from someplace else. Of course, 'cept the Injuns. But that's a whole other can of worms." As the man spoke, he waved the garters in his hand. Suddenly, he realized the merchandise was flapping about in the air, and he remembered why he had taken them out of the suitcase in the first place.

"I just saw a great pitch for these. I'm gonna try it in K.C. The ad goes, 'If you wore them around your neck you'd change more often.' Now that's great copy. What do ya think?"

Elias made no response.

"Don't ya get it?" chuckled Scott, who was quite pleased with his slogan. "See, if you wore this darn contraption where it could be easily seen, you would have to wear a clean one every day. Well, seen or not, any well-dressed gentleman knows ya need several pairs. That, my friend, is called good grooming."

Elias's blank stare was a bit disheartening to the enthusiastic salesman, but he just shrugged his shoulders, tossed the garters back into the suitcase and slammed it shut. "Oh, well," he muttered, "at least it was good practice for Birenbaum's. Old Abe is the one who counts. He's my best client in Kansas City."

As soon as Elias heard the name Birenbaum, he sat up straight in his chair and started pointing to himself.

"Birenbaum! Birenbaum!" he shouted and the Yiddish poured out of his mouth. He tried to make the salesman understand. He stopped and started again. Ever so slowly, he enunciated each syllable and the salesman watched in fascination.

At the end, Mr. Scott slapped his knee once more. "Couldn't make head or tail out of that one," he admitted laughingly.

Frustrated, Elias grabbed the front of his own jacket and pretended to be sewing a button on it. Then he pointed to himself and shouted, "Elias. Birenbaum. Elias. Birenbaum."

At first Scott didn't understand. But Elias persisted and suddenly the salesman cried out, "Yes. I get it now. You're a tailor. You're going to work for old Abe. Well how do you like them apples?"

The salesman told stories all morning long. Except for a familiar word here and there, Elias didn't have any idea what he was saying, but Mr. Scott had an entertaining way about him and the one-way conversation helped to pass the time.

At noon, Scott invited Elias to join him in the dining car. Uneasy around food not prepared in a kosher kitchen, Elias would eat only an apple and a couple of carrot sticks.

"You foreigners certainly have funny eating habits," commented Mr. Scott while he licked his fingers clean of greasy fried chicken. As he watched the salesman scoop up the last mouthful of biscuits with gravy, Elias craved his own mother's home cooking. How long would it be until he tasted her cheese blintzes or her potato pudding or her freshly baked challah again? What was he doing in this strange place?

After lunch, Mr. Scott and Elias returned to their seats and Mr. Scott announced he was ready for a nap. He unsnapped his suitcase and pulled out two small pillows. One he offered to Elias.

He observed how Mr. Scott carefully positioned the pillow between the window and the back of his chair and then snuggled up to it. In a few moments, the salesman was fast asleep.

Elias tried to follow his example, but without Mr. Scott to distract him, he couldn't help but worry about tomorrow's outcome. "I must have been out of my mind to lie to those Galveston agents. Why should Birenbaum show up for me? I wonder if I even have enough money to get back to Texas?" He slipped a hand into his pocket to check on his money. He decided it would be safer in his inside pocket. As he tucked the bills away, he felt Lieberman's gold watch.

Elias pulled out the timepiece, and examined it closely. "If no one will hire me, I'll sell it for a ticket back to Gomel." His eyes began to fill up with water. As much as he wanted to run home, the thought of failing his family was unbearable. Tears slowly trickled down his cheek. So no one would see, he buried his wet face in the pillow.

But the next morning when they pulled into Kansas City, his spirits had changed once again. Hadn't Debra invited him to her new home? So what if Birenbaum didn't need him. Surely, there would be another shop looking for a good tailor. After all, this was the United States of America—home of the free and the rich!

With a positive attitude, Elias stepped down to the platform. Mr. Scott was right behind him and tapped Elias on the shoulder.

"You want to have a doughnut with me before we split up? There's a place inside that makes the best in the territory." He pretended to be eating and pointed to the station.

Adamantly, Elias shook his head and pointed to the ground. Then he put his hand up to his forehead as if he were looking for someone.

"Oh, you've got relatives picking you up," said Scott. "Well, sure that makes sense. Now listen. Good luck and keep your nose clean, young feller." They shook hands and Archibald T. Scott went on his way.

Fifteen minutes passed. The crowds had scattered. A policeman approached Elias.

"Are you waiting for someone?" asked the officer.

Elias shook his head as if to say he didn't understand.

"Well, then get going," he ordered Elias, chasing him away with his billyclub. Frightened, Elias followed a woman up a stairway into the main station. As he hurried behind her, he fumbled in his pocket for the scrap of paper with Birenbaum's address.

A man running to catch his train bumped into Elias and knocked the paper out of his hand. Elias didn't realize he had dropped it, until he went over to a ticket teller to show him the slip.

"Birenbaum's?" he asked and opened his hand. The teller looked down at the empty palm and shouted, "Don't ask me for a handout, buddy. I got barely enough myself."

When Elias saw the slip was missing, he rushed back to retrace his steps. He tried to stay calm while his eyes scanned every inch of the station floor.

He spotted the paper at the top of the stairway and ran over to get it. When he straightened up, Scott was there, munching on a doughnut.

"Well, howdy-do again. I thought you had kinfolks comin' to get you. And what were you doing down there anyways? Did you lose somethin' after I told you about keepin' things in your pockets? Well, don't say you haven't been warned."

Elias disregarded the babble and held out his hand. Scott recognized the address at once.

"Well, I can take you there. It just so happens Birenbaum was going to be my first stop today. C'mon. The trolley car is out that door." Mr. Scott took Elias by the elbow. Somewhat embarrassed to need an escort, he was still secretly relieved to have Mr. Scott by his side.

The streetcar was a five-cent fare and Mr. Scott tossed two nickels into the glass bin. Elias went to pay with his dollar bills but Scott motioned for him to put the money back.

"You save that. You're gonna need it, young feller." As they rode up the street tracks, Mr. Scott tried to point out places of interest, but Elias didn't understand. Besides, it was more interesting to listen to the vendors hawk their wares and the newsboys shouting from the street corners. "Two cents a copy," they yelled.

"Two cents a copy," Elias repeated under his breath. He didn't know exactly what he was saying, but he saw that it attracted the people who stopped and bought the morning paper.

He also watched the street cleaners. Elias did not envy

their job. He hoped he would never have to spend his days shoveling up horse manure.

The ride did not last long enough for Elias, but when Scott hopped off the car, Elias was right behind him. They walked a few blocks. Determined not to miss anything, Elias kept twisting his head from side to side. He saw kosher butcher shops, bakeries, restaurants, a drugstore, a candy store, a fish house, a shoemaker, fruit stands, and a livery stable. Dairymen, icemen, and junk peddlers drove along in their wagons. The streets were full of activity.

They turned the corner and Mr. Scott pointed upward.

"We're here," he shouted. "See. The name's clear as day. BIRENBAUM'S." Elias stepped out to the curb and looked up at the bold letters on the front of the three-story brick building. The salesman opened the heavy wooden door for Elias. "Well, my boy, it looks like you're about to begin to make your fortune in America."

Elias slowly approached the doorway. The nervous teenager from Gomel would have been content to remain outside a bit longer, but the salesman, eager to commence his own day's business, used the end of his suitcase to push Elias forward. The unexpected jolt in the seat of his pants made Elias trip through the doorway.

"Come on, lad!" he heard the voice behind him yell. "In this country, time is money." The man's tone was more than effective. Elias automatically stepped to the side and watched the salesman go to work. "Good day to you, Sir," the salesman greeted the clerk standing at the front counter.

"Why, hello, Mr. Scott. Haven't seen you in these parts for a while. Just the other day, Mr. Birenbaum was saying how you were due for a visit. And let me tell you, it's not too soon! Those collars you left last time went like hot cakes."

"That's what I like to hear! So where is the fine proprietor of this establishment?" Without waiting for an answer, the exuberant Mr. Scott heaved his big suitcase onto the counter.

Immediately the clerk put up his hand to stop the salesman. "Don't waste your time unfastening those locks," he warned. "Mr. Birenbaum had to step out for a while. But he should be back pretty soon, I imagine."

"Well, isn't that how it always is," sighed the salesman. "You rush like the dickens and end up waiting just the same. Oh well. Maybe I should make my other stops and come back later. What do you think?"

The clerk paused. "Whatever suits you, Mr. Scott. We're open till six, and I know Mr. Birenbaum will be mighty glad to see you."

While the two gentlemen continued to speak, Elias could not resist roaming through the aisles. On one counter he saw dozens of embroidered handkerchiefs daintily displayed. On the next were suspenders and bowties. There were white linen blouses with puffed sleeves, elaborately carved tobacco pipes, ladies' purses, brass-handled walking sticks, silk parasols, jewelry boxes, hand mirrors, hairbrushes, combs, ribbons, hats, and more—much, much more. Elias stood there in amazement. He couldn't decide where to look first.

"Mama's eyes will pop out of her head when she sees so many pretty things," he muttered to himself.

Elias was too preoccupied to notice the staircase at the rear of the department store. Otherwise, he would have seen a delicate blond-haired girl staring down at him from the top of the stairway. After a few moments, Rebecca Birenbaum quietly tiptoed down the massive steps and began to follow Elias around the main floor. It was only when the boy picked up a hand mirror and looked at himself that he noticed two large blue eyes studying him from behind.

Elias immediately set the hand mirror on the counter and started back toward the salesman at the front of the store. Mr. Scott was still debating whether he should wait a bit longer or return that afternoon.

The boy never looked over his shoulder. But as he approached Mr. Scott, Elias knew that the blue eyes were still following him.

"Well, how are you, Miss Birenbaum? Everytime I see you, you look prettier and prettier," the salesman exclaimed as he tipped his hat.

Slowly Elias turned around to see the proprietor's giggling thirteen-year-old daughter.

"Thank you. Sorry that my father's not here. He rushed down to the train station. Something about a tailor coming up from Galveston. Of course, Papa was pretty—"

Before the young girl could complete her sentence, the salesman gave Elias a slap on the back and announced, "Oh, I could have saved him a trip. This is the young feller. Don't know a word of English, though."

Rebecca turned to Elias. "Are you that tailor from Russia?" Elias nodded with a grin. The blond-haired girl had spoken to him in Yiddish.

Elias introduced himself and Rebecca explained that her father had gone to the train station to meet him. "But, no doubt, when he doesn't find you, he'll head back here."

No sooner were the words out of her mouth than Mr. Birenbaum pulled open the front door. Mr. Scott snatched the handle to his suitcase and rushed over to the boss.

"Hello there, Mr. Birenbaum! Almost gave up on you." The salesman was smiling from ear to ear.

Normally a very friendly man, Abe Birenbaum waved his hand as if to brush the salesman aside.

"Come back later, Scott. Can't be bothered with garters right now."

The corners of Mr. Scott's smile began to droop. "Sure. Sure. I can always rearrange my schedule for you, Mr. Birenbaum."

Birenbaum regretted his gruff manner and softened his tone. "I'd appreciate it. It's been one of those mornings, if you know what I mean." As he heaved a big sigh of fatigue, the store owner removed the wire-rimmed glasses hooked around his ears and started rubbing his eyes. When the frames were back in place, he extended his hand to the salesman. "I'll make the order later this afternoon. Hopefully, my mind will be clearer."

Scott's smile returned. "You bet," he replied while shaking Birenbaum's hand. "By the way, your new tailor seems like a nice young man."

Birenbaum's mouth opened. "What do you know about this tailor business?"

"Well, sir," boasted Mr. Scott, "I rode in with the young feller from Galveston. He's standin' by Miss Birenbaum, over there." The moment the salesman's finger went up in the air, Birenbaum twisted his head to see exactly who had caused him so much worry that morning. He stormed toward the boy and began ranting in Yiddish.

"What is the funny business going on with the Bureau down there in Galveston? I never said anything about taking a tailor. How did they get it in their heads that I need another name on my payroll?" The furious Birenbaum suddenly stopped to take a hard look at the immigrant standing in front of him.

"You're only a boy."

"Seventeen," Elias assured him.

The store owner looked skeptical. "That's still a boy to me. Listen. I don't blame you. I understand you have no choice in the matter. You go where they send you. But I'm no charity! I'm trying to run a business, and right now I have no openings for a tailor."

Elias's eyes grew misty.

"Please, I'm not heartless," moaned the Kansas City merchant. "I won't throw you out in the street. I'll put you on the next train back to Texas. Surely one of those agents can find you a position in another city. This country is big. It's full of opportunity."

Elias was shaking his head adamantly when Mr. Scott yelled out from the doorway.

"I'll let you two fellas gab away in your Jewish talk. But I'll be back later, Mr. Birenbaum. I got to tell you I think it's a mighty admirable thing you're doin' for this young feller. I mean, we all need a helpin' hand sometime. And just imagine comin' all the way across the ocean and can't even speak the language. Well, you're gonna be blessed in heaven for your good soul. Yes, siree . . ." The salesman tipped his hat and strutted out the door. Abe Birenbaum threw his arms up in frustration.

"All right. All right," he mumbled in Yiddish. "I'll find you something."

5

Elias Cherry, This is Your Lucky Day

THE MOMENT HER FATHER AGREED, Rebecca started to giggle. "I knew you would never send him back, Papa. If you could have seen yourself when you stormed out of here this morning. My goodness you were angry! But you'd never turn your back on one of the immigrants."

Birenbaum eyed Elias and moaned, "How can I? If our own government has given its stamp of approval to the Galveston Movement, how can we Jews not help these poor people?"

Elias wished they would talk in Yiddish. He heard the word Galveston and paled. They're sending me back, he thought.

Birenbaum saw the change in Elias's complexion. "What's the matter, son? You didn't pick up some disease on that ship, did you? Look, I want to do right by you but I can only do so much."

The sound of Yiddish brought the color back into his

cheeks. "Oh, no sir! I'm strong as a horse! Any job you've got for me, I can handle."

"Good. 'Cause there's plenty to do. Now, come!"

Elias followed Birenbaum up to his office on the third floor. Rebecca trailed behind them. Elias was curious about the American girl and every so often turned around to look at her. Each time she giggled.

"Rebecca, stop playing games back there," Birenbaum told his daughter. "I want to hear about Elias. Where is the rest of your family?"

"My uncle contracted traucoma on the ship and they wouldn't allow him into the country. Papa and Mama are depending on me to send for them as soon as I've earned enough money. Mr. Birenbaum, I'm so grateful to you."

"Don't be thanking me yet. You'll have to earn your keep. But before we get started, tell me straight. Is it really Cherry? Usually Russian names are a mile long."

Elias confessed that the inspector in Galveston had had difficulty pronouncing Cherevnosky. "So he shortened it," the boy said, and shrugged.

"What nerve!" cried Rebecca. "Because one stupid man can't sound out four syllables, he doesn't have the right to destroy a family name. If I were you, I'd—"

"Rebecca!" screamed her father. "You are not this young man. Please don't put any foolish ideas in his head. He's going to have enough problems as it is." Then Birenbaum turned to Elias. "If Cherry is written on your paper, then Cherry it is. I myself think it's a fine name. Short and sweet. Easy to spell."

Elias looked from the father to the daughter. He didn't want to offend either. "To be truthful," he said, "I never considered the possibility of a new name until a friend of mine on the ship mentioned that a more American-sounding name would be useful. I guess that's why I didn't object in Galveston."

"You did right," agreed Birenbaum. Rebecca continued to mutter under her breath, but Abe ignored her. Finally, he said, "Enough of this nonsense! Rebecca, back to your geography homework. I don't see why the teachers had to have their confounded conference today. Children should be in school, learning something, instead of pestering their parents all day long."

Rebecca nodded obediently and started toward the door. Suddenly she stopped, turned, and looked straight up at Elias. The girl made no attempt to mask her mischievous smile. "See you later, CHEREVNOSKY!" she blurted out before running down the hallway.

Even Abe Birenbaum couldn't help laughing at his daughter's obstinance. "That one's got a mind of her own," he chuckled.

"Yes, sir," agreed Elias who was becoming more and more interested in the golden-haired beauty. "Girls seem different here."

"Yes, maybe that's the problem," sighed Birenbaum. A moment later he declared, "Okay. Let's get down to business."

The job was not exactly what Elias had expected. Birenbaum made it clear he did not need another tailor.

"But I'm quite capable," Elias pleaded. "I'm the fourth generation of tailors in my family."

"I'm sure you are. But this position is not to sew clothes. Now do you want it or not?" Elias nodded and Birenbaum handed him a mop.

On that one day alone, Elias mopped the floors, washed the windows, hauled heavy boxes of merchandise up and down the steps, and cleaned out the storeroom. Then Birenbaum instructed him to shine the brass bannister by the center staircase. Elias began on the main floor and worked his way upward.

At the top of the second landing, he thought he heard the "humming" of a sewing machine and followed the familiar sound to the end of the hallway. The door to the tailors' shop was slightly ajar, and Elias peeked inside.

The size of the room surprised him. It was small, really not much larger than his father's shop in Gomel. There were other similarities, too.

"Papa would approve," Elias said softly as he checked out each item on the neatly arranged worktable. He saw the spools of thread lined up according to color, boxes of buttons marked by size, scissors in their cases, containers of needles and bobbins, and a big, fat pincushion. Elias smiled when he saw the tailors at their machines, with tape measures hanging around their necks and a piece of marking chalk sticking out of their top pockets. "Just like Papa," he chuckled.

But some things were different. There were so many kinds of fabrics. Bolts of materials stood upright against every wall; Elias eyed the velvets, satins, brocades, linens, and silks with fine appreciation. Seldom did his father ever work with such luxurious fabrics.

However, it wasn't the expensive materials that impressed Elias most. It was the orderliness of the room. Jacob Cherevnosky had taught his son: "You can tell a good tailor by his surroundings. If he keeps a sloppy shop, he sews a sloppy suit." Elias was convinced that these men were two very fine tailors.

Suddenly, one looked up and saw Elias. He smiled.

"Can I help you, young man?"

Embarrassed, Elias shook his head and ran back to the staircase.

To make it really shine, Elias had to polish the brass bannister a couple of times. The chore required a lot of energy and he built up a good sweat. He wasn't quite finished when Rebecca came skipping down the steps. She was holding an orange in one hand and an apple in the other.

"You must be starving," she called out to him. "Papa gets so involved with the store that he forgets to eat lunch. Unfortunately, he doesn't realize that other people do get hungry during the day."

The moment Elias saw the fruit, he realized that he hadn't eaten anything since early morning. As if on cue, his insides began to make loud, gurgling noises. Elias turned red, but Rebecca acted as if she hadn't heard a thing.

"Here. They're for you."

"Thank you! But I don't need both." Elias grabbed the apple from her hand and crunched into it immediately. After he swallowed the first bite, his face lit up with a smile. "It's delicious."

"You take the orange, too," insisted Rebecca. Ignoring the boy's protest, she dropped it inside the big pocket at the bottom of his apron. "My father says fruit keeps you healthy. Nowadays, with pneumonia and cholera, you've got to be mighty careful. You must dress warm and get a lot of sleep, too."

It just then dawned on Elias that he had made no plans for food or lodging. He had no idea where he was supposed to sleep that night. "I must find Shlomo and Debra," he said under his breath.

"What's that?" asked Rebecca who had been watching Elias eat the apple.

"Oh, nothing," he answered quickly.

"I don't mean to be rude," Rebecca suddenly blurted out, "but are you really seventeen years old? You're tall enough, I guess, but somehow you don't seem—"

"And how old are you?" interrupted Elias.

"Thirteen."

"Well, don't worry. I'm older than you. In Gomel, everyone agreed that I was already a very capable tailor. I'm no schoolboy, I assure you," he boasted.

"I still don't think you look much older than the boys in my class."

"You study with boys!" gasped Elias. "At home girls don't even go to school."

"In Kansas City, there are even lady teachers," boasted Rebecca. "That is until they get married. Then they stay home."

"It sounds peculiar to me."

"Not as peculiar as Russian girls who learn nothing at all."

"I didn't say that. There are tutors. But most are trained by their mothers. Doesn't your mother teach you?"

"My mother is dead," replied Rebecca.

Elias bowed his head. "I'm sorry." An awkward silence passed. "I'd better get back to work," he said as he fumbled in his box of rags for a clean cloth.

"But Papa wants to see you in his office."

Once more his palms started to sweat and his stomach began to ache. Had Birenbaum reconsidered? Would he send him back to Galveston? Elias suddenly realized no one had mentioned his salary.

"Well, let him fire me," muttered Elias. "But he'd better pay me for today. These people are not going to treat me like a slave!" He entered Birenbaum's office with that same boldness with which he had addressed the Galveston agent.

Abe Birenbaum looked up from his papers. "All right. I talked to my brother-in-law. He owns the hardware store across the block. Above it, he rents out apartments, and it seems, Elias Cherry, this is your lucky day. One of his tenants just left without notice. So, he says you can have the apartment. Since the boarder had already paid for the next four months, you can have the place rent free for a while. In addition, I'll start you at six dollars a week."

Elias could hardly speak. "How can I ever thank you?" His face lit up with appreciation.

"Just work hard and be on time. I expect you here eight to six, Monday thru Saturday."

"But what about Shabbat?"

The question startled Birenbaum. After a moment's pause, the successful businessman said slowly, "Son, you're smack in the middle of the United States of America. When people here talk about Sabbath, they mean Sunday."

"But you're a Jew."

"And proud of it. But business is business. You're in America. Some of the old ways just don't belong. Well, do we have a deal?" Birenbaum extended his hand.

Elias took a hard gulp before reaching out. As he shook hands, he found the courage to ask, "Does every Jew work on Saturday?"

"Look," shrugged Birenbaum, "I've got two fabulous tailors. Both Jewish. One insists he has to go to *shul* on Saturday mornings. So he only works five days, and I pay him less. Normally, I wouldn't agree to such a deal, but he is worth pampering. On the other hand, it does not take that much talent to mop floors and wash windows. Understand?"

"Yes, sir," Elias said, his head slightly bent.

"Good. Now my brother-in-law, Gus, is waiting for you.

Friday is payday, but here's a dollar in advance. I don't want you to starve before the end of the week."

"But I didn't finish the railing."

"That can wait. You get over to Gus's now."

Rebecca, who had been eavesdropping at the open door, suddenly shouted out, "Papa, can I go, too? I haven't seen Uncle Gus in a long time and I can introduce Elias."

"Sure," said Birenbaum, and motioned for them both to be on their way.

Elias didn't bother to take off his apron. He grabbed his coat, cap, red scarf, and bag and raced after Rebecca. Once outside, Rebecca pointed to a street sign on the corner.

"IN-DE-PEN-DENCE AV-E-NUE," she said slowly. She had to yell over the noisy rattle of passing horses and carriages. "That," she continued in Yiddish, "is your new address."

"Independence Avenue," Elias repeated easily. The boy paused to look up at the sign. "Does it mean anything?"

Rebecca smiled. "Yes, it means freedom." Elias lingered by the sign a couple of seconds more. "Come on," said Rebecca. "Let's cross."

Before they had reached the doorway, Rebecca spotted her Aunt Ethel waving to them from inside the hardware store.

"Hello, Aunt Ethel." The woman turned her cheek toward her niece and Rebecca dutifully pressed her lips on it. "I didn't know you were here today."

Ethel Steinberg ignored the comment as she examined Elias. "Well, at least he looks cleaner than most. Some of them are so dirty!"

Rebecca cringed. Once again she wondered how this woman maintained such a glowing reputation in the community. Throughout the city, Ethel Steinberg was known for her dedication to the United Jewish Charities, the organization that provided free medical services, night school, childcare, lectures, concerts, and a long list of social services for the arriving immigrants. Year after year Ethel Steinberg served on committees and raised money for the needy. Yet this same woman who pleaded on behalf of the world's less fortunate would never have considered inviting an immigrant to her home or becoming good friends with any. She wanted to help them, but from afar. This attitude disturbed Rebecca, but she knew better than to challenge her Aunt Ethel.

"Where's Uncle Gus?" Ethel Steinberg pointed to the counter at the other end and Rebecca gestured for Elias to follow her. But Mrs. Steinberg put her arm out to stop him.

"I just wanted to tell you you'll find groceries up in your cabinets and coal in the stove. It's starting to get pretty chilly at night."

"You're very kind," answered Elias. "Thank you."

"Well, I imagine it's doubly hard for a young man on his own. All of a sudden you've got to cook and clean and care for yourself. What you need to do is find yourself a bride." Ethel suddenly realized she might have offended him. "I beg your pardon. Perhaps you have a young sweetheart waiting in Russia."

Elias giggled as he shook his head.

"Well, don't worry. There are a lot of pretty girls in the neighborhood. I'm sure you'll find someone to suit you."

Rebecca returned with her uncle by her side and announced, "This is my Uncle Gus." Steinberg reached out for Elias's hand.

"Gus Steinberg. Welcome to Kansas City, Mr. Cherry. I'll show you upstairs in a minute."

"Well, Cherevnosky," Rebecca said, "you're on your own." She turned and started toward the front door, but Elias's voice stopped her.

"Won't I see you tomorrow?"

Rebecca shook her head. "Unfortunately, I have to go to school," she said, and she waved good-bye.

Through the windowpane, Elias watched Rebecca cross the street. It took Uncle Gus a couple of tugs at Elias's elbow to get the boy's attention.

"This way," he ordered.

The stairway to the apartment was in a narrow alley at the back of the building. As they climbed the wooden steps Uncle Gus explained, "Now, the bathroom is outside in the hall. I know it's not private, but it's better than an outhouse in the back. All three apartments share the one toilet, sink, and tub, so I advise you to get along with your neighbors. On this side are the O'Reillys. A nice young couple. They just had twin girls. It might be a little noisy at night," he chuckled. "On the other side is an old Italian widow, Mrs. Belluchi. She mostly stays inside. Come. Let me show you around."

After a quick tour of the furnished apartment, Elias was sure he had misunderstood. When he saw the two bedrooms, dining room, kitchen, living room, and back porch, he assumed he would be sharing the space with Mrs. Belluchi and all the O'Reillys. After all, in Gomel, his whole family shared a single, tiny room in the back of the shop.

"No," Steinberg assured Elias, "this is for you alone."

The moment his new landlord closed the door behind him, Elias ran through the rooms once more. He couldn't believe his eyes. He had a feather bed to sleep on and there was a stove filled with coal in the dining room. He checked the cabinets for food. Everything was in place, just the way Mrs.

Steinberg had promised. With a burst of energy, he opened his bag and began to unpack the few items of clothing his mother had sent along with him from Gomel. He whistled and hummed and danced around the apartment, celebrating his unusual good fortune.

"It's all going to be just fine," he kept repeating in his head. Carelessly, he pulled out a loose woolen sock. He had forgotten about the photograph of the family tucked inside. The picture frame slipped out of the sock and fell on the wooden floor. Elias stopped whistling. For some time, the boy stood there studying the familiar faces underneath the broken glass. In the privacy of his new home, he had no reason to hold back tears. His sobs were loud and full of loneliness.

6

Night School

SEVERAL MINUTES LATER, someone was knocking on his door. Elias dried his eyes on his sleeve as he reached for the knob.

"I believe my husband forgot to mention something," announced Ethel Steinberg from the hallway. Elias motioned for her to step inside, but the woman didn't pay any attention. She was too intent on talking.

"I don't know how Gus could have overlooked it. I'm sure when he closes this evening, he'll be more than happy to take you himself."

Elias looked confused. "Where?"

"Why to the Settlement House. One thing you can be sure of. In this town, the Jewish community has always looked out for its own." Suddenly, Mrs. Steinberg was reciting the history of one of her favorite topics—the United Jewish Charities of Kansas City. She rambled on about the Hebrew

Ladies Aid Society, the General Men's Relief Fund, the Bertha Haas Shoe Fund, the Sophie Newgass Sewing Circle, and the Council of Jewish Women. Very tired, Elias tried to look attentive. But none of these Kansas City names had any meaning, until he heard one he recognized.

"And about a year ago, fortune truly smiled on us. We hired Jacob Billikopf."

"Yes," said Elias, "they mentioned him in Galveston."

"That doesn't surprise me," cackled Ethel. "The young man is making quite a reputation for himself here in town. Of course, some of the queen bees were upset to have an outsider meddling in our affairs." The woman leaned forward and whispered, "He came here from Milwaukee. But let me tell you," she argued, wagging her finger in the air, "a trained professional is exactly what we need. And the people love him. Well, like most of you, he's also from Russia. Came here as a poor boy. So, who's better for the job? Well, you can make up your own mind tonight when you meet him. I'm sure you'll want to begin your studies right away."

At the suggestion of school, Elias wrinkled his nose. "I won't have time for *cheder*. I've got to work and earn money," he said defiantly.

The woman jerked backward. "Of course, you must work! Who said anything to the contrary? But my dear boy, education is the key to your success in this country. You must go to night school and learn to read, write, and speak English as quickly as possible. That is why school is absolutely essential!"

Elias, who had never been too keen on school during the day, doubted he would like classes at night any better. But he certainly did not want to antagonize his boss's sister-in-law. With a little prompting from the relatives, Abe Birenbaum might decide to send him back to Galveston. Then how would he escape the perils of Memphis? Fortunately for Elias, Ethel Steinberg just went right on talking.

"I suppose you just misunderstood. No need to be ashamed. You'll see I'm right. Besides, a young man like yourself needs company. Plenty of young people over there."

Suddenly, Elias perked up. "Will Rebecca be coming?" he asked.

"Certainly not!" the woman barked at him. "The Kansas City youngsters have their own schools. What a silly idea to think that Rebecca would ever study at the Settlement House with the immigrants. But don't worry. My Gus will get you all straightened out."

Elias hoped his expression did not betray him. How dare this woman suggest he wasn't good enough to study with Americans. But he prudently said nothing.

Although he had reservations about night school, Elias was indeed eager to see more of Kansas City. Besides, the apartment was lonely. In his first letter home, he planned to write, "You will love this house. It's so big. It just needs a family to fill up the space."

The Settlement House didn't have that problem! The Jewish Educational Institute buzzed with activity day and night. To Elias's delight, the sounds of Yiddish were everywhere. That first evening Gus Steinberg guided the boy through the noisy hallway to find Billikopf.

"Sorry, sir," a tall, skinny man apologized. It was David Kaplan, Jacob Billikopf's assistant. "Mr. Billikopf already left for the evening. But I'll be more than happy to show Elias around our facilities." The offer satisfied Steinberg who had his wife's brisket and mashed potatoes on his mind. The hungry man wished Elias good luck and hurried home to dinner.

The assistant was just starting to tell Elias about all the programs available, when a voice called out to him.

"Elias Cherevnosky?"

The boy turned abruptly. "Shlomo!" The two brawny males threw their arms around one another.

The assistant stood there clasping his hands. "It's so nice to see old friends together again."

Shlomo's booming laugh ran through the halls. "I think you'd call us new friends. We met on the ship from Bremen."

The man glanced over at Elias. "But that means, you only arrived in Galveston a few days ago." Kaplan looked confused. "No. It can't be," argued David Kaplan while thinking outloud. "Mr. Billikopf keeps strict accounts of all our newcomers from Galveston. I may be incorrect, but I'm sure we didn't receive an Elias Cherry on the list from the agents in Texas."

"Well, of course you didn't! My friend was supposed to go to—"

Before Shlomo could pronounce "Memphis," the English teacher took her place outside her classroom and began to ring the school bell. The lobby emptied quickly. Shlomo wrapped his bulky arm around his friend and led him to the door.

"My brother-in-law says night school is fun," groaned Shlomo playfully. "We'll see if Yussell knows what he's talking about. Come on. Debra's inside." A perplexed David Kaplan was still scratching the top of his curly head as Shlomo and Elias disappeared into the classroom.

Yussell Resnick was right. English class was a lot of fun and certainly different from Morton Lieberman's classroom in Gomel. The teacher, Miss Goldstein, was lively, creative, and amusing and could make the most tedious exercises into a challenging game. Also, Elias was relieved to see that she never used a strap to punish the students.

After their first class, he confided to Shlomo, "When I first took my seat, I felt foolish in a class taught by a woman, but Miss Goldstein is wonderful."

"And pretty, too," added Shlomo with a wink.

Debra overheard the remark and said, "Don't get any ideas. Yussell told me Miss Goldstein is engaged to David Kaplan. She's almost a married woman."

Shlomo snapped his fingers and grinned at Elias. "Oh, well. Her loss, I guess."

Debra ignored her brother's snickering. "So what happened, Elias? How did you get here? Where are you living?"

"I told them I wanted to go to Kansas City and they put me on a train. Just wait until you see my apartment." Elias told them about his arrangement with Abe Birenbaum's brother-in-law. As Shlomo listened his eyes opened wider and wider.

"Where is this palace?" he boomed.

"In-de-pen-dence Av-e-nue," Elias answered slowly, as he visualized the sign on the corner.

Debra and Yussell started to laugh. "That's our street, too," Debra told him. "We live above the drugstore, down the street from Birenbaum's."

"Of course with three of us, it is a bit cramped. We'll be looking for something larger soon, I'm sure," Shlomo added.

Debra started to shake her head. "Tsk. Tsk. Listen to my brother. A few days in America and he already talks like a big shot."

"Why not?" demanded Shlomo.

Debra put her hands on her hips and exclaimed, "How quickly we forget, Shlomo Zusstovetch. All your life you prayed that the roof wouldn't leak at night while you slept on a cold floor."

Reuben and I did the same, Elias thought to himself.

"Well, never again!" shouted Shlomo. "Our world has changed!" he yelled triumphantly.

"Only in some respects," Debra replied. Her mood changed. "Not everything can be discarded so easily."

Shlomo stamped his foot in frustration. "Even your husband agrees that some of the old customs will only hamper our progress here. Why must you be so stubborn?" He turned to Elias and complained, "Debra cannot accept the fact that we are forced to work on Saturdays. But if we refuse, they will replace us. Tell me, is there a choice?"

Elias shrugged. "To be fair, the agent in Gomel warned me. I just hoped I might be one of the lucky ones."

Shlomo tossed his arm around his buddy. "You're lucky just to be here. Don't make any demands."

Elias saw the pained expression in Debra's eyes and remembered his own mother's reaction.

"I don't understand. You know very well that Jews are not to work on the Sabbath," Dena Cherevnosky had reprimanded the agent in Gomel.

"It's different in the West. Many are not observant. But don't think they don't care about Judaism. Giving charity is ingrained in their lives. Otherwise, this program could not work. They hear about the pogroms. They know they have a responsibility." The agent had said these words as if he had spoken them a hundred times.

Dena had turned away in disgust, but Jacob had disregarded her disapproval. "If need be, Elias will work on the Sabbath," he had assured the agent. "And when I arrive, I will do the same."

"I don't want to hear such things," the wife had screamed, running out of the shop. In Debra, Elias saw his mother's own heartbreak, and as they all walked home together, he decided it would be best not to tell his family about the work on Saturdays.

I'll tell them everything but that, he thought as they turned the corner to Independence Avenue.

When she wished him good night Debra added, "You must come to our home every Friday night for Shabbat dinner. That much we can still do."

"Thank you," replied Elias who was sure to mention the invitation in his first letter.

He also wrote about all the hard work at Birenbaum's. That first week, he tried so hard to impress his new boss. Usually by mid-morning he had worked up a healthy sweat. It discouraged Elias to think his efforts were going unnoticed. More than anything, he wanted to prove himself so that he might be allowed to assist the two tailors. He didn't realize Birenbaum was watching his every move.

"Let's face it," the store owner confided to his brother-in-law after Elias's second day on the job, "I don't know this kid from Adam. He could steal me blind."

"Why, Abe, this Cherry fella seems all right to me," said Gus. "Anyways, I thought the Galveston agents were supposed to check these people out."

"Well, that's what's troubling me. I mean he seems like a nice kid. Hard working and all that. But the way he showed up here out of the blue. I can't put my finger on it, but something smells fishy."

"Oh, you're such a Nervous Nelly!" Gus chuckled. "After all, you only have him washing windows and scrubbing floors. How much trouble can he cause?" Abe nodded in agreement but still he kept an eye on Elias.

Two days later, he watched Elias carry a bolt of imported silk cloth up to the stop. As Elias started up the stairway, Birenbaum called out to him from the second floor.

"Cherry! Keep it steady."

"Don't worry, sir. I carried heavy bolts for my papa all the time in Gomel. Of course none were as beautiful as this."

Mr. Birenbaum proceeded downward. "Young man, with hard work and determination, you too will be able to afford such luxuries."

In the middle of the wide stairway, Elias stopped beside his boss. "To tell the truth, Mr. Birenbaum, I don't really care about buying such things for myself. But I'd sure like a chance to sew them."

Birenbaum smiled and thought for a moment before he answered. "I'm a fairly direct man myself, so I respect your candor. But what I said the other day still stands. I don't need someone to sew clothes for me. I have two fine tailors up-stairs. Now, I gave you a job and found you a place to live. I really don't know what more I can do."

"Oh, Mr. Birenbaum, you know I'm grateful."

"Well then, my suggestion to you, young man, is to work hard, save your money, and study English. Once you bring your father over here, the two of you can start your own shop. You won't need mine. But you must know how to read and write."

The advice didn't make his janitorial duties any easier. But night school took on a new meaning and from that day on, Elias became Miss Goldstein's most dedicated student.

Besides their regular drills, in November the class studied about the Pilgrims landing at Plymouth Rock. The day of

Thanksgiving had held special significance for all the immigrants who had suffered the injustices of religious persecution and looked to America for a new beginning. After just one week in Kansas City, Elias was about to celebrate his first holiday in America.

On the Wednesday before Thanksgiving the Settlement House canceled all regular activities to host their annual Thanksgiving party. Elias was especially grateful. The promise of a kosher turkey dinner with all the trimmings made his mouth water. Except for his first Friday night meal at Debra's, his diet in Kansas City had consisted mostly of bread, crackers, cheeses, fruits, and vegetables. At night Elias dreamed about his mother's thick potato soup and the tangy aroma of her delicious stuffed cabbage. Even if he had known any recipes, Elias never would have considered cooking for himself. First of all, he was too tired after ten hours at Birenbaum's and another two hours at night school. Besides, in Gomel, the kitchen was a woman's domain.

After work, Elias raced across the street to change for the holiday dinner. He had one suit. Actually it was his father's, but Dena had insisted he bring it to America. He had outgrown his own Bar Mitzvah suit months ago.

"Even if we are poor, why should a tailor's son walk around with sleeves up to here?" she had asked, pointing to her elbows.

As he examined the handsome outfit, Elias was happy his mother had forced him to take it. He ran out to the hall bathroom to wash up before dressing.

When he saw the closed door, he knocked impatiently. A minute later, Mrs. Belluchi slowly turned the doorknob. The old woman looked up at the youth and smiled.

Gripping a sturdy black cane in her right hand, Mrs.

Belluchi moved slowly down the corridor. She reminded Elias of many elderly customers in his father's shop. He found himself helping the old woman to her door. "Thank you," she said before stepping inside. Then Mrs. Belluchi rested her wrinkled hand on the boy's soft cheek and blessed him in Italian. As soon as she shut her door, Elias raced back to the washroom.

He washed his face and scrubbed his hands several times as he checked for grit underneath his fingernails. Then he looked up at the wooden medicine cabinet and inspected himself in the mirror.

"I need a haircut," he moaned out loud. In Gomel, his mother had nagged him about such things. Now that he worked at Birenbaum's where all the clerks were so well-groomed, Elias was growing self-conscious about his own appearance.

"You're maturing," Dena would have told her son.

With a wet comb, he tried his best to slick down the dark, wavy curls, but the thick mane of hair did not respond. He grimaced at his image and tried several more times. He thought he had finally succeeded, but a minute later the curls bounced up again. He gave up on the hair and in-spected his teeth. Smiling at himself in the mirror, he decided his dark brown eyes with their long, black lashes comple-mented his large white teeth rather nicely.

"Remember to smile a lot," he reminded himself.

Finally, he examined his jaw for facial hair. None had grown. Elias heaved a sigh of disgust. "Baby cheeks," some of the older boys in Gomel had labeled him. Still, Elias was pleased with the reflection in the mirror. If only his curls would stay in place.

The suit made up for any imperfections. Even Gus

Steinberg, who happened to see Elias running down the back stairs, was impressed.

"One thing for sure!" laughed Gus. "You don't look like a stock boy tonight. I like that suit."

"Thank you," answered Elias with a big grin. "My father made it."

"Can you sew like that?" Gus asked in amazement.

"Almost as well." Elias tried to sound modest.

Gus Steinberg shook his head. "I don't know why Abe is wasting your talents."

Elias smiled. The comment had boosted his high spirits even more. "If Mr. Birenbaum should need a tailor, I'm always ready," he said cheerfully, and started down the alley.

7

Rats in the Cellar

ELIAS WALKED OVER to Adler's Drugstore where he was supposed to pick up Shlomo. He found his friend at the end of the soda fountain slurping up the last sips of a chocolate phosphate. When Shlomo heard his name called out, he spun around on the stool. "What are you doing?" cried Elias. "We're about to have our first Thanksgiving feast and you're filling up on seltzer!"

"In honor of the holiday, Mr. Adler's pretty daughter treated me to a soda. How could I refuse?" Shlomo winked at the chubby teenager working behind the counter. She giggled.

Elias nodded politely at the girl and then leaned over to whisper in Shlomo's ear. "Come on," he said impatiently. "I don't want to miss any of the meal."

"I think she likes me," Shlomo said as they walked over to the Settlement House.

"Who?" said Elias.

"Lucy. Lucy Adler. The druggist's daughter."

"How do you know?" Elias asked.

"I just know," grinned Shlomo.

Lately, Elias had been thinking about girls, too. At work he often watched the young ladies browsing through the store. He had decided none were half as pretty as the golden-haired Rebecca Birenbaum. Every day he hoped she would come running through the front door.

"Hey, do you want to race?" challenged Shlomo.

Before Elias could protest that they shouldn't run in their good suits, Shlomo was charging down the empty block. Elias could not resist and chased after him. As they approached the Settlement House, the two were laughing and running side by side. Both were breathless but grateful to have the other's companionship.

Elias and Shlomo lingered beneath the gas streetlight outside the building. They removed their overcoats and readjusted each other's bow tie. Elias was still straightening Shlomo's collar when a carriage pulled over to the curb. She did not see him, but Elias watched Rebecca, along with her Aunt Ethel and another boy, step down from the buggy. He waited for them to walk inside before letting go of Shlomo's shirt.

"Well, it's about time," complained Shlomo. "Come on. We're going to turn into icicles out here."

The lobby was jammed with people. Elias scanned the faces but did not spot Rebecca anywhere. From a far corner he saw Debra and Yussell wave to him. The boy flashed them a big smile and then turned in the other direction. He noticed the door to the dining room was slightly ajar. Somehow, he managed to squeeze through the crowded foyer to the doorway.

He peeked inside and recognized many customers from the store. He counted at least a dozen ladies scurrying around the room, making sure all the table settings were complete.

Then he noticed Rebecca. She was helping her aunt spoon out cranberry sauce at the buffet table. As the girl worked, a charm from her dainty bracelet kept dangling into the food.

"Get that jewelry off your wrist," Elias heard Mrs. Steinberg tell her. He watched Rebecca undo the clasp and drop it into a side pocket in her bright yellow calico apron. When she looked up, she saw Elias staring at her.

"Hi, there, Cherevnosky!" Rebecca giggled as she walked over to greet him.

"Good evening," he answered in English.

"Very good," she praised him in Yiddish, "but you really shouldn't be here. Can't you see we're not ready? My aunt will never forgive you if you let the others in here too soon. She and her committee have planned this dinner for months!"

Elias pointed to the door. "But it was open." Then he stepped inside and closed it. "Now no one will come in," he announced.

"All right. You win, Cherevnosky," flirted Rebecca, who couldn't help but admire how handsome Elias looked in his suit. "But anyone who stays must work," and she pointed in the direction of the kitchen.

Elias didn't care. Helping was a good excuse to spend more time with Rebecca, and the ladies were relieved to have a strong pair of arms to carry the heavy platters of food. Meanwhile, they insisted Elias sample all of the new recipes. Elias was more than happy to accommodate them. But the boy who had followed Rebecca into the building was not so friendly. He never budged from his place. When Elias asked Rebecca about him, she made a face.

"That's Aaron. Aunt Ethel's fifteen-year-old nephew from St. Louis. His family comes every Thanksgiving. He was supposed to help us with the trays, but now that you're here, I guess he figures he can sit around and loaf," she said in a loud voice.

"That's right, Becky," he jeered. "I'm a man. I don't do *woman's work!* Besides, what do you care? You've got someone to do your bidding." He glanced down at the seat beside him and noticed an apron lying over it. It was pink with ruffles. "Hey, Bud," he shouted to Elias, "I think you forgot this." He threw the frilly apron at Elias. Elias turned red and Aaron burst out laughing.

"Don't pay attention to him," said Rebecca. "Come on, Aunt Ethel wants us to open the door."

As soon as he saw his friends, Elias introduced Rebecca to Shlomo, Yussell, and Debra, but a few seconds later she excused herself to help the other ladies at the buffet table.

Shlomo elbowed Elias in the side. "I saw you sneak in here. I thought it was the food. But now I understand," he chuckled.

Everyone ate and drank heartily. As the wine started to take effect, song and laughter filled the air. A robust, bearded man stood up on his chair and raised his glass high. A hush fell over the room.

"The Czar thought he could destroy us with his pogroms, but tonight we have the last laugh. On this evening before Thanksgiving, we remember the Pilgrims who came here like us in search of freedom. That first year, it was the Indians who taught the English how to survive. For us, it is our friends at this Settlement House and all the Kansas City men and women who support the United Jewish Charities. Bless you all. *L'chaim.*"

The crowd cheered and the ladies, who had worked so hard to make the evening a success, searched for their lace handkerchiefs to pat the corners of their eyes.

As soon as she could sneak away from her aunt's side, Rebecca joined Elias at his table. Shlomo insisted that she hear their famous "cockroach story." Just as they had done on the ship many times, the two boys reenacted their heroic deed. Elias wasn't quite finished with the story when Aaron marched over to the group.

"Aunt Ethel expects you back at the buffet table at once," he said, poking Rebecca on the shoulder.

"Why?" the girl said, turning around in her chair. "There's no more to do right now."

"I guess she doesn't like you sitting here," he answered belligerently. "And maybe she does need your help."

Rebecca stood up and defiantly slipped out of her apron. She shoved it into Aaron's arms. "You haven't lifted a finger since you arrived. You go to the buffet table. Do a little work for a change." Rebecca sat down and turned to Elias. "Please finish," she said sweetly to Elias, ignoring the boy fuming behind her.

After the story Rebecca cringed. "What a horrible experience. I hope I never have to suffer in a place like that. You all must have been desperate to leave if you would tolerate that disgusting boat."

"We had no choice," answered Debra. "The pogroms are devastating."

"Why doesn't anyone fight back?" Aaron sneered in English. "Sounds like they're all cowards." He didn't expect any of the greenhorns at the table to understand him. He took a sudden step backward when Yussell Resnick stood up and looked him in the eye.

"Defenseless people cannot challenge barbaric murderers," the cabinetmaker said in Yiddish. "They come racing through the streets on wild horses, trampling over young mothers, small children, and old men hobbling with their canes. The Cossacks burn our homes and shatter our storefronts. No Jew is safe."

Rebecca opened her eyes in horror. "Is it really like that?" she asked Elias.

The boy picked at his piecrust with a fork. His voice quivered as he spoke. "You never know when it will happen. People always die. Once they almost shot me."

"No!" gasped Rebecca.

Still staring down at his unfinished dessert, Elias swallowed hard. "Hannah Shiffrin saved me," he said softly.

"Is that your girlfriend?" teased Aaron.

"Aaron!" cried Rebecca. Although her tone suggested she would never have asked such a personal question, Rebecca, in fact, was eager to hear Elias respond. She sometimes worried that Elias was only being attentive because she was the boss's daughter.

The question had made Elias smile. "If you must know, Hannah was four years older and never paid any attention to me. But our mothers were friendly. Mr. Shiffrin was already in New York."

"But what happened? How did she save your life?" asked Rebecca.

Elias paused a moment. He looked from face to face and knew they were all waiting to hear. "Well," he began slowly, "it's just as Yussell said. First they came galloping through the streets. The madmen on horses were everywhere. People, young and old, were screaming, running for their lives while shattered glass crunched under their feet. I remember I was standing by the side of road, watching in horror. I knew I had to run but my legs felt like two blocks of cement. I couldn't move. Then, suddenly, a hand gripped my arm from behind."

"Was it a Cossack?" cried Rebecca.

"No. It was Hannah. 'Let me go! Let me go!' I kept shouting until I realized she wasn't one of them. We ran to the rear of her family's shop and Hannah pointed to this narrow door at the back of the store."

Aaron, who was still hovering over Rebecca let out a loud sigh of disgust. "Hey, Cherry, why don't you just tell everyone that you hid in a closet for two hours and stop being so dramatic." This time they all understood because he spoke in Yiddish.

"That's not what happened at all," Elias told them.

Rebecca twisted around in her chair and glared up at Aaron. "You're such an embarrassment," she whispered to him in English. "If you've got to breathe down my neck, keep your big mouth shut and let Elias tell the story." She turned back and smiled politely, "So where were we?"

Elias continued. "Hannah opened the door and I followed her down a flight of wobbly steps to her basement. It really smelled down there. The place reeked of mildew." Elias cringed as he recalled the stink. "But that wasn't the worst part. Hannah told me there were rats in the cellar."

"Oh, no!" gasped Debra, who had been bitten by one as a child.

"For a few minutes, we stood there in total silence. But imagining I heard a rat, I completely lost my nerve and decided that I'd rather face a Cossack than to have a set of teeth digging into my flesh. 'I don't want to stay here,' I started screaming, but Hannah refused to let go of me. Then we heard the glass crash above us. The voices became louder and louder and we both stayed perfectly still." Elias paused as he visualized every detail. "Someone kicked open the basement door and the footsteps came closer and closer. Suddenly, a piercing scream filled the air. I watched the Cossack look down at his boot. Trapped underneath his thick heel was the tail of an angry rat. I tell you its teeth glistened in the dark."

"Did it get the Cossack?" cried Shlomo.

"No. The other way around. His pistol shot brought the others to the doorway. 'Don't worry!' he yelled up to his friends. 'The rats will take care of any Jews down here.' They looted the store and left."

"Is that all?" cried Aaron. "Why it sounds to me, buddy, like a rat saved your skin."

"No. It was Hannah," he said, in a controlled voice. "If she hadn't held on to me, I would have walked right into that mob. They would have killed me for sure."

Rebecca shuddered. "Let's not even think about that. But tell me, what happened to Hannah? Did she ever get to New York?"

Elias nodded and smiled. "Last we heard, she had married and was expecting her first child."

With a big grin on his face, Shlomo slammed his palm down on the table. "That's America for you," he shouted with glee. "Always a happy ending. Come on, folks. Enough of these gloomy stories. We're here to celebrate. He stood up and pulled Elias off his chair. He insisted Yussell stand up, too. Then he ordered them to take off their jackets and join the line of men dancing in the center of the room. Debra and

Rebecca ran over to a circle of women doing a hora. Only Aaron lingered behind the table.

"They all look like clowns out there," he muttered under his breath. Secretly, Aaron dreaded any large social gathering because he was uneasy around strangers. Elias's poise only made Aaron feel worse.

He looked down at the apron Rebecca had shoved into his arms and started to fume inside. In disgust, he threw the apron on the table. Her gold charm bracelet slipped out of the pocket. Aaron saw it and went to drop it back inside, but suddenly an idea popped into his head. Making sure no one was watching him, he slipped the piece of jewelry into Elias's jacket.

"This will teach them both a good lesson," he snickered to himself. As he was turning away from the table, he saw his Aunt Ethel waving to him. She looked very stern.

"I thought I told you I wanted Rebecca to sit with my committee. It's not proper for her to be dancing with those people, and she's paid much too much attention to that Elias Cherry. My friends aren't blind."

Aaron shrugged. "I told her, Aunt Ethel. She wouldn't listen."

"Well, this is an outrage. I appreciated his help before, but I don't want him getting any smart ideas. Go tell Rebecca we're leaving."

The girl begged to stay longer but in a few minutes the carriage was waiting for them outside. Ethel Steinberg stood in the foyer buttoning her coat. She frowned when she saw Rebecca walking to the door with Elias. Just before stepping outside, Rebecca extended her gloved hand. The boy held on to it shyly.

"Happy Thanksgiving, Cherevnosky," Rebecca said with a giggle.

"Thank you. Happy Thanksgiving to you," Elias said proudly in English. As he spoke he felt a funny sensation inside of him. Could he dare hope that this beautiful American girl, whose life was so different from his own, might have secret feelings for him, too? The thought made him blush.

"You're awfully red," Rebecca remarked.

"It suddenly seems very warm in here," Elias answered as he boldly squeezed Rebecca's hand in his.

Now Rebecca was blushing.

A moment later, with her free hand, Rebecca grasped her tiny wrist and began to pull gently away from Elias. She suddenly remembered her bracelet.

"Oh my goodness. I almost left it here." She ran back into the dining hall and spotted her apron on the table. When she reached into the empty pocket, she grew frantic. "It must be here," she repeated several times. Finally, she dropped to her hands and knees to look under the table. Ethel had watched her niece rush into the dining room and hurried after her. As soon as she realized the problem, she searched the apron again.

"Are you sure you put it in the pocket?" asked Ethel Steinberg, who was becoming more annoyed by the minute.

"Yes," moaned Rebecca. Her big blue eyes began to swell with tears. "It can't be lost. That bracelet was Mommy's."

Elias told everyone there that he remembered seeing Rebecca slip the bracelet into her apron. The party came to a halt as folks began to search the room.

Aaron even pretended to help Yussell look underneath the buffet table. After a ten-minute search, the bracelet appeared lost. Rebecca burst into tears, and Aaron decided it was time to initiate Phase Two of his plan. He walked over to Elias who was looking under the buffet table again. Shlomo was also down on his hands and knees.

"Don't waste your time, Cherry. Your pal Yussell and I already combed this area. I have a hunch that we won't find the bracelet because it's not lost at all. I think somebody took it."

"Why would anybody do that?"

"You tell me. You spent the most time with Rebecca tonight, and you're the only one who knew she had stuck it in her apron."

"What are you trying to say?" demanded Elias as he got up to his feet.

"Well, for starters do you have anything in your pocket that doesn't belong to you?"

Shlomo overheard the accusation and jumped up in a flash. He grabbed Aaron by the lapels. "How dare you call my friend a thief?"

"Let go of my jacket," said Aaron gritting his teeth.

"Please, Shlomo," Elias pleaded. "I don't know what he means, but this isn't your fight." Shlomo let Aaron free begrudgingly.

"Oh, so you want to fight?" Aaron fired the question as he threw the first punch. Elias momentarily lost his balance and crashed into the buffet. No one noticed the bracelet drop underneath the table. Elias got right back on his feet and stunned Aaron with a solid punch in the nose.

By then, the commotion had captured everyone's attention. Aunt Ethel gave out a chilling scream when she turned and saw blood dripping down her nephew's chin. Yussell stepped in and stopped the fight.

"He stole the bracelet," yelled Aaron as he pointed an accusing finger. Desperate to prove his innocence, Elias even allowed Aaron to check his pockets.

"But I tell you he had it in his jacket," the boy lied.

It was Rebecca who saw something shimmer underneath the buffet. "There it is," she cried.

"See!" Aaron gloated. "It fell out of his jacket when we were fighting. I knocked him down right on that spot. Yussell Resnick can tell you it wasn't there five minutes ago."

Rebecca did not want to believe that Elias had stolen her bracelet, but when her Aunt insisted they leave at once, she turned without even saying good-bye.

Ethel Steinberg didn't know with whom to be more upset—her niece for being so irresponsible or her nephew for ruining her beautiful Thanksgiving dinner. One thing was certain. An immigrant named Elias Cherry was a troublemaker. She intended to speak to both her husband and brother-in-law about this ingrate to whom they had shown so much kindness.

"Don't think this incident will go unnoticed," she threatened as she rushed out the room.

Elias returned to Independence Avenue with a ripped suit, a swollen face, and an uncertain future.

8

Birenbaum's Decision

THANKSGIVING DAY TURNED out to be gray and cold. The dreary weather outside was a perfect reflection of Elias's dismal mood as he remained inside his apartment. After last night's ordeal, he suspected that neither Abe Birenbaum nor Gus Steinberg would want anything more to do with him.

"If I have to, I'll sleep on Yussell's floor. And if there's nothing else, I'll clean up the horse manure from the streets. But nobody's sending me back to Russia. Nobody!" he shouted at the four walls.

Moments after Ethel Steinberg had stormed out of the Settlement House, almost everyone had begun to whisper in small groups. Elias hadn't been surprised to see the Kansas City matrons huddling in a corner, but he never imagined that fellow immigrants would turn against him.

"That boy's a disgrace," a woman informed her friends.

"Shh," whispered another. "He's standing right behind you."

"I really don't care if the no-goodnik does hear me," she replied in an even louder voice.

"But how do you know he took it?" demanded a stocky man who had chatted with Elias several times at night school and liked him.

"Don't you understand? It doesn't matter whether he did it or not. The fact is, he shouldn't have been so familiar with that American girl. We're strangers here. People can interpret things however they like. What if they decide we're all thieves. What then?"

While the others echoed, "You're right, you're right," one person suggested, "Maybe they should ship him back before there's any more trouble."

The woman who had started the conversation liked that idea. "You can be sure the Czar knows how to take care of his type," she cackled.

Later that afternoon, as he climbed up the back stairs of Mr. Adler's drugstore, the vicious laughter still rang in his ears. At the top of the steps, Elias knocked on the Resnicks' door. Earlier that week, Debra had invited her friend to share Thanksgiving dinner. Now, as he waited at the doorstep, Elias wondered if Debra and Shlomo agreed with the others.

Thoughts of being both friendless and penniless in a country where he understood so little made Elias feel faint. He leaned against the side of the house for support; the boy was still a little dizzy when Shlomo appeared.

"Well, there you are! We were afraid you might not come." Shlomo put his strong arm around Elias and led him inside.

"I almost stayed home," Elias admitted to his friend. "To be honest, I'm not in a very festive mood. You'd probably have a better time without me."

"Nonsense!" scolded Debra from the dining table. She was checking that everything was in place. "Aaron is a liar! That's all there is to it. I didn't like him from the moment I set eyes on him. But let me tell you, I don't plan to let him or anyone else spoil our first Thanksgiving in America. It's our holiday, too!" For the first time that day Elias actually smiled.

The four of them sat down to a scrumptious feast. Unlike the traditional American meal served the previous evening, Debra's turkey dinner included a raisin-and-apple noodle kugel; a prune, carrot and sweet-potato tzimmis; and a heaping platter of extra large liver kinishes. To Elias, it smelled, tasted, and felt just like home.

One thing was different. Except for *kiddush* on Shabbat or religious holidays, Elias did not drink alcohol in Gomel. At first Elias was hesitant to join his friends in a glass of blackberry wine, but Shlomo convinced him that a few sips would relax him. After the first glass, the liquor kept tasting better and better.

With two bottles of wine soon empty, everyone started behaving a bit silly. Yussell burst out in song with Elias whistling in the background. Debra marked the time by clapping her hands and moving her head from side to side. Their impromptu performance inspired Shlomo to stand up and make a toast.

"A million times, Lord, thank you, thank you, thank you. Our troubles are finally over!" Although Shlomo's voice sounded a bit tipsy, his words had a very sobering effect on Elias. Suddenly the fourteen-year-old's eyes filled up with tears.

"I'm not sure what will happen tomorrow when I walk into Birenbaum's." Elias's voice cracked as he spoke. "There's a good possibility I could lose my job on the spot. That means I won't have a place to live either." Elias paused to get control of himself. He did not want to sob in front of everyone.

"Then you will stay with us," said Debra who would never forget Elias's kindness on the ship. She looked across the table at her husband. Yussell cleared his throat, as he gripped Elias's shoulder. "It's useless to try to guess what will happen. But I do think these Americans are good people. We'll just have to wait and see."

Elias excused himself right after dinner. He claimed he needed a good night's sleep. Debra made no effort to detain him, but at the door, she reminded Elias that Hanukkah would begin that weekend.

"On Sunday I'll make potato latkes. You come and we'll light the candles together." Her voice was extra cheerful.

"Sure," mumbled Elias.

That night sleep did not come easily. Still agonizing over the unlucky turn of events, the boy tossed back and forth on his pillow into the early hours of the morning. Throughout the night, Elias kept checking Lieberman's pocket watch to see how much time was left until morning. Finally, a couple of hours before dawn, Elias fell asleep. Yet even that brief rest was not meant to be an escape. He woke in a cold sweat, still seeing the terrified look on little Reuben's face before him.

In his dream, Elias and his brother were sailing together from Bremen. Reuben insisted on sitting on top of his big brother's broad shoulders. Just as Elias was boosting his brother upward, a giant wave crashed against the side of the ship. Elias lost his balance and Reuben toppled over the railing.

Elias reached out to save his brother. Groping at the empty air, he woke up with a start. He jumped out of bed and in his bare feet ran out into the cold, dark hallway to the bathroom. He splashed several handfuls of icy water over his face. Then he looked into the mirror of the medicine cabinet.

"No matter what," Elias said to the reflection in front of him, "you cannot fail the family."

During all those weeks of preparation, Elias had repeatedly assured his father that there was no reason to worry about him. "Of course, I'm old enough," he had told his father more than once. Never did Elias even hint that he was scared.

But late one night, about two weeks before his departure, Elias remembered, he had lain awake next to his brother Reuben, listening to the sweet, steady rhythm of the younger child's breathing. Thoughts that he might never see his family again suddenly overwhelmed Elias. Just when he was about to rush out and tell his parents he could not go with Lieberman, Elias had overheard his father talking to his mother.

"Oy, Dena, Dena. How can we send our child halfway around the world? I look at him and I see he's as big as I am, but in my head, I know he's only a little boy."

In the dark Elias could not see his mother reach out to his father. But he heard the gentle kiss and her reply.

"Customers are always commenting on how so young a boy can be such a skillful tailor. The truth is, this child has been studying your every move since he took his first few steps. I don't think he was more than six when Elias told me how he always watched you very carefully, because one day his papa would need his help." Dena heaved a heavy sigh. "Well, Papa, I'm afraid that day has come."

Elias sobbed bitterly over the sink for several minutes. Piercing screams coming from the hallway suddenly distracted him. Elias wiped his eyes. He recognized that sound. Like an alarm clock, the O'Reilly twins wailed every morning at seven o'clock for their first feeding of the day. Elias heaved a deep sigh. The waiting was almost over.

Fifty-five minutes later, Elias marched across Independence Avenue. With new conviction, he walked through Birenbaum's side entrance marked for employees only. He had decided the first thing he must do is face Rebecca's father and plead his case. But as he ran up to the office, one of the tailors grabbed him by the sleeve.

"Can you really sew?" Joe Rothman asked Elias in Yiddish.

"Of course," the boy answered, looking rather startled.

"Well, come on," and Elias followed the man into the tailor's shop.

"Look. My partner woke up sick as a dog today. I went to pick him up as I do every morning, and his wife informed me that Izzy's too weak even to get out of bed. Stomach cramps, chills, the works. And you can be sure he's plenty ill because Izzy Horowitz doesn't want to lose the pay. Face it. We all need every cent."

Not exactly sure what this man wanted, Elias shrugged, "I'm sorry to hear about Mr. Horowitz."

"You're sorry!" he cried. "I'm the one with the noose around my neck. Look, sonny, we've got orders up to here." The man lifted an arm over his head to make his point. "Izzy and I had figured we'd have to put in extra time. During the holidays, it's always crazy. But there's no way humanly possible I can do it all alone. And if we disappoint the customers, well that's that. Word of mouth in this town can make or break a business. So? What do you say? Can you give me a hand?"

"Bu-bu-but shouldn't you talk to Mr. Birenbaum fir-first?" Elias stuttered.

"Sure! As soon as Abe shows up, I'll tell him you've got to help me until Izzy gets back on his feet. Believe me, boychik, there's no time to even think about it. Now come on. Roll up your sleeves and let's get to work."

Joe Rothman marvelled at the boy's ability. Elias explained, "I've been helping my father since I could walk." But for all Joe's flattery, Elias was still anxious about his boss's arrival.

At precisely nine o'clock, the door to the shop swung open. "Where's Izzy?" Abe Birenbaum demanded.

Joe jumped up from his machine. Elias was sure Birenbaum's eyes were fixed on him, but the boy didn't dare look up from his work.

"Listen, Abe," Elias heard the tailor say, "Izzy's caught some kind of bug. The poor guy couldn't get out of bed this morning. But this Cherry kid is a lifesaver. He wasn't kidding when he said he's a tailor."

Suddenly, Abe Birenbaum was speaking in English. Although Elias recognized a word here and there, nothing really made sense. The two men stepped outside and Elias felt the sweat collecting on his palms. Too nervous to continue, he lay his throbbing head down on the sewing table. He never saw the customer enter.

"Hey! Abe Birenbaum said you could fix my suit for me."

Elias heard the voice and lifted his head up. He jumped out of his seat when he saw Aaron standing there holding his suit. The other boy was just as surprised.

"You're still here!" Aaron screamed in Yiddish. "You've got a lot of guts after what happened Wednesday night. Look what you did to my new jacket." He showed Elias the torn seam. "You're just lucky I get this done for free or I'd make you pay for it." He hung the suit on the crowded rack.

"But you started it," Elias protested.

"And you can be certain I'm gonna finish it too," he threatened. "My Aunt Ethel is already making plans to get you out of Kansas City—maybe even the country. As she says, 'Your kind America can do without.'"

"Why do you hate me? What did I ever do to you?" Elias's eyes were filling up again.

"Ah, so now you're gonna blubber like a baby. Well, you weren't crying Wednesday night when you were showing off for Rebecca. Just where do you come off, a greenhorn, making eyes at an American girl?"

"I don't understand," pleaded Elias.

"Well, maybe you'll understand this." Suddenly Aaron jumped at him and pinned Elias down to the floor. Gloating over his easy victory, Aaron laughed in Elias's face. In his own defense, Elias spit at Aaron. Enraged, the St. Louis boy jabbed his knee into Elias's groin. The young tailor screamed out in agony. Satisfied, Aaron got to his feet, while Elias lay there, curled up in pain.

"Well, Cherry, after I tell everyone how you jumped at me again, I wouldn't be surprised if they really do throw you in a paddy wagon. They already know you're a thief."

Elias could barely speak, but somehow he managed to whisper once more, "I didn't take the bracelet."

Aaron let out a howl of laughter. "You know that and I know that," he screamed in Elias's face, "but everyone else is sure you're guilty."

"Not everyone!" a voice called out from the hall. Rebecca marched into the shop and pushed Aaron to the side. She stooped down to help Elias. "Can you move?" she asked gently. Taking the girl's arm, Elias slowly got back on his feet. The smallest movement made him wince, but Elias's pride prevented him from acknowledging any pain.

Rebecca turned to Aaron. "I heard everything, and I'm going to tell my father right now. I can't wait to see Aunt Ethel's face when she realizes I was right about you. You're a big fat liar!"

Aaron sneered at her. "You're fighting a losing battle, Becky Birenbaum. Go ahead. Aunt Ethel won't believe you over me. She's furious with you for being so chummy with this greenhorn in the first place. Say whatever you like! See if I care."

He was halfway out the room, when Aaron suddenly stopped by the clothes rack. He pointed to his suit.

"By the way, Cherry. Keep your grubby paws off my jacket. I don't want any second-rate job."

"Ignore him, Elias!" Rebecca spoke loud enough so Aaron would hear her out into the hallway. Then she turned and in a softer voice said, "I'm going to find my father. Will you be all right?" Elias nodded. He watched Rebecca leave and then carefully repositioned himself at his machine.

When Joe returned, Elias did not mention Aaron's visit, nor did the tailor mention his talk with Abe Birenbaum. Work kept Elias's mind off his troubles and by noontime he was even relaxed enough to laugh at some of Joe's Yiddish jokes. But all smiles disappeared when a clerk popped his head into the doorway and told Elias that Birenbaum was waiting for him upstairs.

Slowly, Elias climbed the steps to the third-floor office. He felt his body trembling all over. Elias clenched both fists to try to stop the shaking. Before knocking on the door, he wiped the sweat off his hands and swallowed hard.

"Come in," Birenbaum shouted. He looked up from his papers and motioned for the boy to take a seat. "Son, this is the busiest season of the year," began Birenbaum. "I don't have any time for nonsense. Now, I gave you a chance—"

"And I'm grateful. I've tried hard to impress you," pleaded Elias.

"And I was impressed until this business with the bracelet."

"I never took it. I've never taken anything that doesn't belong to me. You've got to believe that."

"Well, my daughter does. But Ethel and her nephew are quite adamant that you're the culprit."

"No matter what anyone says, I'm telling the truth."

Birenbaum took a long, hard look at his employee. "Well," he shrugged, "I guess fate is on your side, Elias Cherry."

"What do you mean?"

"This morning when I came to work, I figured the easiest thing was just to throw you out. But the plain truth is no one can prove you stole anything. In this country a man is innocent until proven otherwise. And since I'm desperate for someone to work in the shop with Joe this week, I'm going to take a chance. Of course, I already warned Joe to keep a close eye on you." Birenbaum pointed his finger in Elias's face. "Just one spool of thread disappears and I'll have you working on a chain gang shoveling ditches for the rest of your life. Believe me, you'll wish you had stayed put in Russia!" Mr. Birenbaum paused briefly so Elias could digest his words. Then the man added, "The wages will remain the same. I don't imagine Izzy will be out too long. Then you can resume your janitorial chores."

In tears, Elias bounced up from his chair to shake Birenbaum's hand. "I didn't know what I was going to do," he said wiping his face with his shirtsleeve.

The display of emotion embarrassed Birenbaum. He reached into his pocket for a handkerchief. "Here use this." Then he said, "Son, just do right by me, and we won't have any problems."

"I will never forget your kindness," sniffled Elias.

"I figured I had to do something or I'd never get any work done today. First, Rebecca storms up here in a fit and when I finally get her settled down, this other young woman barges into my office. She claimed you two met on the ship. She told me outright that only a fool would believe Aaron over you."

Elias's eyes opened up in amazement. "That must have been Debra," he said.

"Whoever it was, she certainly doesn't mince words. Listen. I've heard enough about this matter. As far as I'm concerned, it's over and everybody is to get back to work."

Elias returned to the shop, whistling one of his favorite tunes.

"I'm glad you're feeling better." Elias looked across the room and saw Rebecca standing near his sewing machine. She smiled.

"Oy! You mean I got another sick one," whined Joe from his corner.

Elias assured them both he felt just fine and started working right away. For several minutes, Rebecca stood there and studied the young tailor at work. Suddenly, she announced, "I wish I knew how to use a sewing machine."

"Oh, Miss Birenbaum," replied Joe, "you'll never need to worry about such things. No one expects you to be a seamstress."

"But I'd like to be able to sew my own clothes. Papa said my mama used to make beautiful dresses."

Rebecca hoped Elias would volunteer. Elias did not respond, and Rebecca just stood there and pouted. Finally, she turned to go and Elias called out to her.

"I could teach you," he said hesitantly.

Rebecca's face lit up with a big smile. "You've got a deal, Cherevnosky," she called back to him before skipping out the door. Moments later, Joe heard Elias whistling a tune.

"I smell romance in the air," he teased his young associate.

Elias shook his head in denial, but Joe knew better.

"Can't say I blame you, son. She's a pretty one, all right, and full of spunk, too. But a word to the wise! If you want to stay employed, keep your distance. Sure, Birenbaum is a decent man. But face facts. Well-to-do folks here don't raise their daughters to go gallivanting around with poor immigrants. Listen, I've only been in this country seven years myself and every night I thank my lucky stars for men like Abe Birenbaum. But I'm not stupid. If you want to stay friends, don't get too friendly. That's my motto."

"But you were here. You heard Rebecca," protested Elias. "She's the one who asked for help. I was just being polite."

"Do yourself a favor, boychik. Save your manners for the boss. He's the one you've got to please."

Unfortunately Joe was only half right. There was also Ethel Steinberg to consider. In the back of his mind, Elias still worried that the woman would demand he find a new apartment. All afternoon, he was sure that an eviction notice was waiting for him across the street.

Elias didn't have to wait until closing time to face the wrath of Ethel Steinberg. At 2:00 P.M. she arrived at the department store to take Rebecca and Aaron home with her. Before going up to the third-floor office, she walked into the tailor's shop to inquire about Aaron's suit. When she saw Elias, she gasped. The boy froze.

"What are you doing here?" Ethel screeched.

"What do you think? The boy is working," said a voice behind her.

Ethel turned around and saw her brother-in-law.

"But Abe, I thought I had made myself perfectly clear."

"I think you had better have a chat with your nephew, Ethel. Some of the details have changed since yesterday. If I were his father, I'd take a strap to the boy."

Mrs. Steinberg stood there with her mouth open. Elias expected the woman to say much more, but when she finally regained her composure, Ethel Steinberg walked out of the room without uttering a single word. As he examined Elias's work, Birenbaum made no comment about the incident.

"Very nice. Good work, Cherry," is all he remarked before making his exit.

When the other tailor was certain the others were gone, he turned to Elias and winked. "See what I mean? Take my advice, boychik, and you'll have a long and happy career."

9

Ethel Makes Trouble

AFTER A WEEK, Izzy returned to work. The month of December was so busy in the shop that Elias continued to help the two tailors. More and more, Joe and Izzy depended on their young associate, and customers soon began to ask for him by name. Forced to converse with all of them, Elias's English improved steadily. At night school, Miss Goldstein recognized his progress and was quick to praise him.

"It's obvious that Elias uses his new language during the day. You must all do the same, if you expect to succeed like him," Miss Goldstein told her students one evening.

After class Elias had volunteered to erase the blackboards. Shlomo sneaked up behind him. "What's between you and Miss Goldstein?"

"What do you mean?"

"Elias this and Elias that," he mimicked. "If I didn't know

the lady was engaged, I'd say she's got her eye on you, boychik."

"You're just jealous," Elias teased him right back.

"Sure am," agreed Shlomo as he grabbed the eraser from his pal's hand and ran to the opposite corner of the room.

"Okay. Throw it back," Elias laughed. They began throwing the eraser back and forth. This was precisely why Elias liked Shlomo so much. With him, there was always some fun to be had.

Still, even on the Friday evenings at Debra's Elias tried to speak English. Whenever Shlomo would complain his brain was too tired to translate, Elias knew exactly how to embarrass him.

"I thought you were the one set on giving up the old ways. 'Strictly American,' you boasted on the ship."

Debra still spoke mostly Yiddish, but Elias never teased her. After all, it was Debra who had rushed to his defense. At the Settlement House while Shlomo joked with the men or flirted with the ladies, Elias and Debra often talked quietly in a corner. With a blush, Debra admitted to Elias that she dreamed about being a mother. Elias admitted to Debra that he dreamed about Rebecca Birenbaum.

"She likes you too, Elias."

"How can you tell?" he asked.

Debra smiled to reassure him. "I saw the way she looked at you at the Thanksgiving party."

"But we come from such different backgrounds," he sighed.

"Nonsense. She's a Jew and you're a Jew. You're the same."

The last week of 1907 was like a dream come true for Elias. Rebecca was out of school for her winter holiday and came to the store every day. She had not forgotten Elias's promise to teach her how to use the sewing machine, and each afternoon at lunchtime, Elias gave Rebecca sewing lessons.

Even the older, experienced tailors agreed that Becky was a quick learner, but they also knew there was more going on than just sewing. They winked and nodded at one another each time they saw Rebecca smile up at Elias.

On Friday afternoon, Rebecca pulled her father into the shop to show him what she had learned. Abe Birenbaum was genuinely impressed and made a mental note to add a little extra to his young tailor's paycheck.

Everyone was happy except for Ethel Steinberg. That Friday, she was shopping at the store and heard about the lessons from one of the clerks. She stormed out the front door and across the street to get her husband.

"But Ethel, you have no right to interfere," Gus tried to reason with his wife.

"What do you mean?" she roared at him. "Rebecca is your sister's daughter. Your flesh and blood. She has no right shaming the family like this. I can just imagine what people are saying."

"But the child has done nothing."

"Not yet, maybe. But you mark my words. I'm a woman. I know about these things."

Ethel wasted no time in letting Abe Birenbaum know exactly what she thought. She dragged poor Gus over to the department store with her. When she started talking about her woman's intuition, each of the men had difficulty keeping a straight face.

"Laugh all you like! Men are always the last to know in matter such as these. But I'm telling you, Rebecca likes this boy."

"So do I," Abe said with a shrug.

"Enough to be a son-in-law?" screamed the woman.

"You're talking nonsense, Ethel," Gus interrupted. "Rebecca is just a schoolgirl. Marriage is years away."

Ethel Steinberg turned to Abe and looked him straight in the eye. "It's sooner than you think. I'm telling you, Rebecca concocted these sewing lessons as an excuse to spend more time with that Russian."

"So what if that's true?" shrugged Birenbaum. He still could not figure out why he should be alarmed.

"Well! If your daughter has it in her head that these poor immigrants are proper suitors for a girl of her background, then just don't say I didn't warn you." Abe Birenbaum made no effort to stop his sister-in-law as she slammed the office door behind her.

"Forgive her, Abe," Gus apologized for his wife. "You know she loves Rebecca like her own. Can you blame her? The woman just wants the best for the girl."

"Of course. We all do. But I'm surprised at Ethel." Irritation was building in the merchant's voice. "She forgets. I'm the son of an immigrant. German instead of Russian, perhaps. But don't kid yourself. Poverty and prejudice don't change with the language. My parents suffered plenty when they arrived from Frankfurt. My father was a poor shoemaker and my mother scrubbed other people's floors to make a few extra pennies. I always hated the fact they led such hard lives, but I've never been ashamed because they were immigrants."

"Calm down, Abe. I've got no argument with you," Gus replied.

"I'm sorry. Ethel just got me going there for a minute, but I don't want to fight with you either." He put his arm around his brother-in-law and gave him a squeeze. He and Gus had been dear friends since his engagement to Frances, and through the years they had struggled together to build up respectable businesses on Independence Avenue. Abe admired Gus for the same qualities he prided in himself—hardworking, honest, fair, and devoted to family. In his opinion, Gus had made only one serious mistake in his life—marrying Ethel Feld.

"Please, darling, don't be so critical," his wife Frances used to plead with him in private. "My brother Gus is happy. That's all that counts."

Frances showed even more tenderness toward her sister-in-law when it was discovered that Ethel would never be able to bear children. Together, the two young wives worked actively for their synagogue and volunteered for a variety of projects sponsored by the Jewish charities in town. But Frances was always quick to remind her husband that there was one major difference in their lives.

"I've got Rebecca," Frances would say with her beautiful smile. In the next breath, her eyes would look very sad. "Poor Ethel has only meetings."

Then Frances died. Longing for his wife and overwhelmed by the idea that he had a four-year-old to raise all by himself, Abe was deeply grateful for Ethel's devotion to Rebecca. Still, the woman voiced some ugly opinions, and even after all that had happened in their lives, Abe found it difficult to overlook Ethel's snobbish attitudes.

As he walked his brother-in-law downstairs, he assured Gus that he was not angry. Suddenly Abe had a silly grin on his face.

"What's so funny?" Gus asked.

"Oh nothing," Abe said quickly, waving his hand in the air. "By the way, will you and Ethel be at temple tonight?"

"Of course. You know we go every Friday."

"Good. I'll see you there."

Elias was amazed when Birenbaum invited him to Friday evening services at B'Nai Jehudah. The boy doubted that his mother would actually approve of him praying in an American shul where men and women sat together, no one was required to cover his or her head, and services were conducted almost completely in English. But after his employer had just been so generous that afternoon by giving him a bonus, how could he decline the offer? Besides, Elias wouldn't refuse any invitation that meant spending more time with Rebecca. When he told Joe where he was going that evening, the tailor frowned.

"Oy, boychik, remember my motto. You watch yourself."

They arrived at the synagogue a few minutes early. Heads turned as Abe guided the children to the front. After they had passed several rows of people, the whispering began.

"Isn't that the one from Thanksgiving?" the ladies were asking one another.

Elias recognized several customers in the sanctuary. Still, he was conscious of being the only Russian immigrant in the congregation. Whenever he caught someone staring at him, the boy smiled politely, but not everyone smiled back.

Ethel Steinberg, who had not seen them enter, was pleased to hear a voice call out *"Shabbat Shalom, Auntie."* The woman looked up from her prayer book with a pleasant smile.

"Come sit with us, Rebecca," the woman said, tapping the vacant seat next to her.

Rebecca saw only two empty places. "We'll need three, I'm afraid. Papa invited Elias." The young girl pointed to her father who had stopped to introduce Elias to Rabbi Mayer. While praising his young tailor to the Rabbi, Birenbaum put his arm around the boy's shoulder. Ethel turned her head away in disgust, and sat through most of the service gritting her teeth.

Afterwards, she cornered her brother-in-law. At her side was Jacob Billikopf's assistant from the Settlement House.

Ethel spoke in a very low voice. "Abe, this is David Kaplan. Since November he's been helping Mr. Billikopf place the immigrants in town."

Birenbaum extended his hand. "Oh, so you're the rascal who surprised me with young Cherry." The merchant started to chuckle. "That day he showed up, I would have liked your head on a platter. But I've got to admit, things have—"

"That's the point, Abe. The agency never sent him," his sister-in-law interrupted.

"What?"

Kaplan turned red. "Sir, it's most embarrassing. I have no idea how he got to your department store. He wasn't even supposed to come to Kansas City. The men in Galveston list him in Memphis, Tennessee."

Abe looked confused. "Why wasn't I informed earlier?"

Kaplan turned even redder. "Since you didn't complain, I figured I wouldn't upset the applecart. The success of our program depends on good people like yourself. I was worried you'd think we weren't in full control and then want nothing to do with us."

"So why do you pick now to tell me?" barked Birenbaum.

"Well, sir, when Mrs. Steinberg came in this afternoon to tell me about all the trouble, I knew I had been wrong not to come forth sooner. Please, sir, we value your support and generous contributions. If there's a problem, be sure we'll take care of it at once."

When the assistant left them, Ethel put her hands on her

hips. "I hope you enjoyed your little joke tonight. I wonder though, just who's been the fool?"

Abe refused to answer her. He ordered Rebecca to go home with Ethel and Gus and told Elias to come with him in his carriage. The boy felt uncomfortable about riding to and from synagogue on the Sabbath. When he mentioned this to Birenbaum, the merchant snapped, "That's the least of your worries." Elias didn't understand the reason for the curt response, but the boy heard the anger in his boss's voice and was quiet for the remainder of the ride.

When they turned the corner on to Independence Avenue and pulled up to the hardware store, Mr. Birenbaum turned to his employee.

"I heard a story tonight," he said and he repeated what Mr. Kaplan had told him. "Boy, I want the truth and I mean the truth," he said coldly.

"It's very complicated," Elias replied in an unsure voice. "Would you come upstairs?" He began his story with the day, so long ago, that Lieberman had first mentioned the Galveston Movement.

"Fourteen! Only fourteen. I can't believe it," Birenbaum mumbled over and over again as he listened to the entire story in Elias's apartment. When the boy finished, Birenbaum, who was still sitting in his black, felt derby and overcoat, just shook his head in amazement.

"Well, son, all I can say is, if this is another one of your concoctions, you're one heck of a storyteller."

"But that's exactly how it happened," Elias insisted.

"Tell me. Do your parents realize your Hebrew teacher was sent back to Bremen?"

Elias didn't answer right away. Instead he got up from the small, oak dining table and walked over to a kitchen drawer.

He opened it and took out a rumpled piece of paper. Elias placed it in front of Birenbaum.

"The letter came last week. It's my second one."

Abe Birenbaum glanced down at the table and saw the Yiddish handwriting. Then he slid the sheet back towards Elias.

"No, please," the boy encouraged his boss, "I want you to read it."

Birenbaum picked it up and by the dim light of the kerosene lamp, he began to read Jacob Cherevnosky's letter to his son in America.

I almost collapsed in the shop when I saw Morton Lieberman walk through the door. Whatever possessed you to stay in America by yourself, I will never know. We are just thankful that you have been placed with such a wonderful man as you describe your Mr. Birenbaum in Kansas City. I pray he continues to watch over you until we can all be together.

Your mother and I are still furious with Lieberman, but he insists he did you a favor by not forcing you to return on that horrible ship. The stories he tells are frightening, but we suspect he's exaggerating. Unfortunately, he has come back with even more ailments than before and flatly refuses to take the journey to America by himself. Naturally, none of the other families will consider his offer to chaperone one of their sons. They now all know how he abandoned you in Galveston. He claims his remaining funds are very limited (although I am inclined to think otherwise) but he has, at least, agreed to help out with one of our fares, if we can be ready to sail to America this spring.

Please save every penny you can, Elias. I will have to pay back anything Lieberman loans us, and I am certain we will arrive in America with almost nothing but the clothes on our backs. Of course, at this point, I will make whatever promises necessary just so the family can be together.

Believe me, if we had the means right now, your mother, Reuben, and I would be on the next ship to Galveston. I lie awake at night, thinking about you.

Dress warmly and be careful. We boast to everyone how well you are doing in America, but inside, our hearts are crying.

Slowly, Birenbaum looked up at Elias. He said, "You should write your father and tell him not to worry. Tell him he has a very determined son." He smiled kindly at the boy as he said "Good night," from the doorway.

While Birenbaum drove home, he remembered Ethel Steinberg's remarks and became angry all over again. "She thinks she does so much for these people, but I doubt she understands how they suffer. Her only concern is if they look right!" It always annoyed Birenbaum when Ethel and her gossipy friends would comment about each new group of immigrants. Understandably, most arrived wearing ragged, dirty clothes. Many of the peasants from Russian villages had never even seen a toothbrush until they received their first one at the Settlement House. All the children were immediately enrolled in the special classes to learn how to wash properly, as well as to care for their teeth and hair. Usually, it was the youngsters who taught their parents. Although Ethel would frequently remark how "satisfying it was to finally see these unfortunate souls becoming more and more American," Birenbaum suspected that his sister-in-law was mostly interested in their quick progress so that they wouldn't prove to be an embarrassment out in the community.

The scenery outside Birenbaum's carriage started to change. The brown, red, and gray brick buildings with their striped awnings and billboards disappeared. In their place came massive stone and wood homes. Usually returning to these pretty tree-lined streets filled Abe Birenbaum with a personal sense of accomplishment. His address was proof that even a poor shoemaker's son could become a respected member of American society. But tonight, the well-to-do neighborhood was an unsettling reminder that he was, perhaps, just as guilty as Ethel Steinberg. As he approached his stately three-story yellow house with its large, inviting front porch, the department-store owner shuddered. When had he ever taken the time to get to know even one of these immigrants?

He saw his housekeeper, Mrs. Whitehall, waiting at the doorway. She took his hat and coat and he started upstairs. As he did every night, Abe peeked in on his sleeping daughter. Carefully, Birenbaum tiptoed across the hardwood floor towards Rebecca's canopy bed. He glanced down at the child; instantly his somber expression softened into a warm smile.

Standing there and admiring his daughter, it suddenly occurred to Birenbaum that Rebecca and Elias Cherry were just about the same age. At the end of January, Rebecca would also be celebrating her fourteenth birthday. He heaved a quiet sigh as he retired to his bedroom across the hall.

Although his body was weary, his mind refused to drift into a peaceful slumber. For over an hour, Birenbaum kept readjusting his comforter and propping up the stack of goose-feather pillows under his head. All the while, he kept thinking about Jacob Cherevnosky's letter to his son. Finally, his muscles relaxed and the throbbing in his head was replaced with a welcome, drowsy sensation. Before falling into a deep sleep, however, Abraham Birenbaum made an important decision.

10

Curtain Up

ELIAS SUSPECTED Mr. Birenbaum was up to something when that following Thursday afternoon David Kaplan marched into the shop, with a long list of questions about Elias's family. Ever since his confession, the teenager had been worried that Birenbaum would reveal his secret to authorities in Galveston who would then force him to return to Gomel. This sudden interrogation seemed to confirm his worst fear.

"After all this time, why do you ask these questions?" Elias demanded in English. Although he had been repeatedly addressed in Yiddish, the immigrant had insisted on answering like an American. His words were clear and his sentences complete. Still, Elias could not control the trembling in his voice.

The worker from the Settlement House just kept scribbling notes on his tiny pad. Out of frustration, Elias finally slammed his fist on the sewing table. "What is this all about? I've done nothing wrong," the boy pleaded.

Kaplan half smiled. "No reason to be alarmed, Elias. These questions are simply routine. We just like to keep our records complete."

Elias wasn't satisfied. He had begged Birenbaum to keep his secret confidential. He waited for Kaplan to leave the shop, and then jumped up and ran out the door. "I'll be back in a moment," he yelled to his co-workers as he leaped out into the hallway.

At the stairway, he looked below to see if Birenbaum was out among the customers. When he didn't spot him, he rushed to the third-floor office. Elias took the Kansas City merchant by surprise.

"Don't be ridiculous. No one is forcing you to go back to Russia," Abe had to reassure him several times. "Obviously, none of the agents suspected your real age in Gomel or Galveston. But that no longer matters. You're here now, and no one in his right mind would suggest you return to those murdering Cossacks. We're not ignorant in America. We know what's happening."

Elias bowed his head. "I'm sorry," he mumbled. Embarrassed by his outburst, Elias started for the door.

"Wait!" Abe ordered. Elias turned once more and saw Birenbaum rummaging through his desk drawer.

"Here it is," Birenbaum announced and he handed Elias an envelope. "Rebecca insisted I deliver it to you personally."

Elias still felt uncomfortable and quickly excused himself. He rushed toward the stairway, looking at the pink envelope in his right hand. He stopped by the bannister, and tore open the seal. The note was in Yiddish.

Rebecca Anna Birenbaum kindly requests the pleasure of your company at her fourteenth birthday party on Sunday, January 26 at 2:00 P.M. She looks forward to greeting all her guests for ice cream and cake.

Elias read the message several times. Its formality seemed odd, but the thought of going to Rebecca Birenbaum's home thrilled him. As he slipped the card back into its pretty pink envelope, he felt a hand tapping him on the shoulder. He twisted his head to the side and saw Birenbaum. The boy jerked backward.

"Didn't mean to frighten you, son. After you walked out, I remembered I was supposed to tell you that I'll come get you on the day of the party. Becky is only worried you'll get lost. Of course, we've got plenty of time to make arrangements. Better get back to work now. I don't pay you good money for standing in the hallway."

"Yes, sir," Elias replied, and he practically flew down the stairs.

When he came back to the shop whistling, Joe winked at Izzy. "Aren't we in a fine mood," laughed Joe.

Elias held up his invitation and proudly recited the inscription. Izzy smiled, but Joe shook his head. "Don't say I didn't warn you. You know how I feel about mixing with these rich Americans. Mark my words. It always spells trouble."

"Joe! Let the boy be," said Izzy. "He's young. He needs to have some fun." He turned to Elias. "I understand these parties can be very fancy. The sweets. The decorations. And don't forget the balloons. Oh, and of course, the presents. Everyone will be bringing something for the birthday girl."

Elias frowned. "I hadn't thought about a present."

The tailor rolled his eyes. "Oy, some can be very extravagant." Elias groaned.

"Don't be foolish!" cried Joe. "No one expects you to waste any money on such nonsense."

"Of course!" Izzy agreed. "I didn't mean that you had to buy a gift. Just go and have a good time. It seems to me the best present you can give that girl is just showing up. I'd say she has a real crush on you."

Elias blushed even more when Joe asked, "What's wrong, son? Your two cheeks look like they're on fire." The older tailors enjoyed a good laugh, and Elias returned to his sewing table to avoid any more discussion. Still, for the rest of the day he couldn't stop thinking about a present for Rebecca.

At ten minutes before closing, Elias finished for the day. He quickly tidied up his space and hurried down to the main floor. Roaming the aisles always reminded him of his first day in Kansas City. The fancy merchandise still impressed him. But today one item in particular caught his eye. The clerk saw Elias coming toward him and smiled.

"Done early, eh?"

Elias nodded. The boy was pleased with himself for understanding the man's English. Then he pointed to a very dainty figurine on top of the case. "The cost, please?" he asked slowly.

The clerk turned and looked above him. Carefully, he brought down a porcelain figure of a young girl holding a basket of flowers. Her long hair was yellow and she was wearing a pale blue dress.

"Isn't she pretty?" commented the clerk. "And look!" The man behind the counter flipped the figure upside down and demonstrated how to wind up the music box.

While the clerk bobbed his head from side to side to the

lively tune of "Oh Susanna," Elias again inquired, "The cost, please?"

"Oh, of course. Two dollars."

The music came to an abrupt halt and Elias walked out of the store discouraged. Deep down, he knew he shouldn't spend even a nickel from his savings. Certainly, he was in no position to squander two dollars of a week's wages. Yet, the desire to give Rebecca something special for her birthday nagged at him.

Elias raced off to night school. "Debra will probably have a good idea," he consoled himself as he pushed against the brutal wind. But only Shlomo was waiting for him in the lobby.

"Where's Debra? She inside already?"

Shlomo shook his head. "Debra's not coming tonight."

"Why not?"

"Too tired. And this morning, she had a stomachache. Yussell stayed home with her. It's a good thing, too. That wind is wicked."

Elias nodded that he agreed, but he didn't bother to hide his disappointment.

"Something wrong?" Shlomo asked.

Figuring that Zusstovetch would tease him like the tailors, he merely shrugged, "What should be the matter?"

"Good. 'Cause I've got a surprise for you." Shlomo held out his hand. "Want to go see a show?"

Elias recognized the orange tickets and screamed with delight. For the moment, at least, he forgot about a present for Rebecca Birenbaum.

During Elias's first month in Kansas City, Yussell had taken Shlomo and him to the Pantages Theater. Neither of them had been able to follow the subtitles to the silent movie, but the classic melodrama with its sinister villain, delicate damsel in distress, and brave, rugged hero required no translation. What had really impressed Elias was the piano player, who at the front of the theater had played right along with the movie.

Elias had liked the vaudeville show that followed even better. Naturally, every time a pretty girl appeared, Shlomo had elbowed his pal, Elias, next to him. But Elias had been fascinated by it all and walked out wondering what it might be like to perform on stage.

"Listen! It won't cost us a cent," Shlomo boasted. He flipped over the two stubs and Elias saw the four letters in bold red print. He still couldn't read much English, but he recognized "FREE."

"Where did you get them?"

"Lucy Adler gave them to me. I think the girl wanted me to take her. They're only good for tonight. But when her father saw us laughing over at the soda fountain, he came over to inform her that she had to stay late to help him in the store." Shlomo had that devilish grin on his face. "These American girls may be a lot bolder than our girls back home, but," he groaned, "you can be sure that fathers are the same on both sides of the ocean."

Silently, Elias blessed Mr. Adler for being so protective of his chubby little Lucy. "So, what's the movie? Who are the acts?" Elias's excitement was obvious as the questions rolled off his tongue.

"Who knows? Who cares?" shrugged Shlomo. "It's free!"

They still attended their English class, but Elias and Shlomo sat in the back in order to leave early. In their excitement, even the blustery cold did not bother them. When they spotted the theater at the end of the block, they raced toward the box office. Together they looked up at the marquee but the words AMATEUR NIGHT meant nothing to either one. Still certain they were in for a good time, the boys handed their passes to the usher in the lobby.

"To the back," a deep voice ordered. Shlomo made a face, but Elias grabbed his friend's arm and pulled him away.

"What did you expect?" Elias whispered. "They don't give away the best seats for nothing."

The theater filled up quickly. Elias checked Lieberman's pocket watch and realized the show would start any second. He noticed two empty seats in the second row and nudged Shlomo. "I wonder why no one sat up there."

"'Cause that's where we're supposed to be." Shlomo jumped up to claim his rightful place. Unsure, but still laughing all the while, Elias followed his friend's bold lead.

They plopped themselves down in the front section. Immediately, Elias felt uneasy. The people around him were different from the rest of the audience. One nervous-looking woman was clutching a violin case. A scrawny young man had a wooden-headed puppet resting on his lap, and a toothless old man was holding a box of spoons.

Elias tugged at Shlomo's sleeve and informed him that he was going back to their seats in the rear. "I don't think we're supposed to be here." Elias was already on his feet when the house lights dimmed and the music began.

"Hey Bud, you're blocking the stage," an unfriendly voice yelled from behind. The master of ceremonies appeared and the boy sat down again.

"Tonight, folks, it's all homegrown talent as the Pantages Theater presents its new weekly Amateur Night. Any soul daring enough to hop up on this stage and sing, dance, tell a story, or just make a plain fool out of himself could go home with this." The smiling host held up a crisp five-dollar bill and the audience applauded wildly. "That's right! One of our lucky acts sitting right here in the first two rows will be five dollars richer by the end of this evening."

"Let's get out of here," cried Shlomo.

"No," Elias said defiantly. "I think we should stay."

"Didn't you understand? They expect us to entertain them."

Elias leaned over and whispered in Shlomo's ear. The red-head let out a big boom of laughter. "Why not?" he continued laughing. "After all, this is America. Anything's possible."

Most of the acts were quite good. Elias and Shlomo applauded loudly for the old man who played "Dixie" on the spoons. But they both grew increasingly nervous when the skinny ventriloquist panicked in the spotlight.

"Hey, get the two dummies off the stage," someone yelled from the balcony. The audience hissed and booed and suddenly everyone was chanting, "Give him the hook!" A long red hook appeared from one side of the curtain. In another second it would have been wrapped around the man's waist, if he had not run off screaming in the other direction. Even Elias couldn't help but laugh as the audience hooted with delight.

Then it was the boys' turn and they took center stage. As they had done so often, Elias and Shlomo re-enacted their famous cockroach escapade. Many in the audience were immigrants and fully appreciated the horrendous conditions suffered by steerage passengers. Elias did most of the talking and managed to tell almost the entire story in English. The few times he had to resort to a Yiddish phrase, some members of the audience yelled out the translation. But his imitation of Lieberman discovering the insect and collapsing onto his meal was so humorous that no one cared if the boy was struggling at times.

Shlomo, a natural clown, outdid himself in the roles of the fat cook and drunken sailor. His pratfalls were as comical as those of any real vaudeville performer. The audience cheered wildly, and the master of ceremonies insisted that the two young men take several bows.

Afterward, the old spoon player was called up to accept the prize for first runner-up. He was slowly making his way to the front, when the host made the announcement.

"And our grand prize winners—Sam Zussman and Elias Cherry." Like two bolts of lightning, the boys were back on stage, collecting the five-dollar bill. Shlomo had at least a half-dozen ideas for how to spend his portion of the winnings. For Elias, the choice was simple. The next morning, Elias walked into Birenbaum's and proudly purchased the porcelain figurine.

Izzy chuckled quietly when he saw his young associate walk in and set the gift in the far corner of the room. Joe sighed in disgust, but after a signal from Izzy, kept his mouth shut. Still bubbling over with excitement from the previous night's victory, Elias revealed all. At the end of his account, both men applauded.

"Well, when you first came in here," Joe admitted, "I was ready to chew you out for spending money you didn't have. Now that I know the whole story, I want to be the first to congratulate you."

"Besides," said Elias, "I still have fifty cents," and he stood up and jiggled the coins in his pocket. Like two proud uncles, Joe and Izzy boasted about their talented associate to everyone. But they weren't the only ones to publicize Elias's triumphant evening.

The next week, Joe ran into the shop waving the newspaper high in the air. The Pantages Theater had placed a prominent ad in the *Kansas City Star* to promote their new amateur night on Tuesday evenings. In the advertisement, the management congratulated Elias Cherry and Sam Zussman for taking first place in the past week's talent contest.

Elias kept checking his pocket watch every hour on the hour. He was anxious for the work day to end. He could hardly wait to show the clipping to Shlomo so that they could bask in their glory together at night school. But Shlomo had other things on his mind that evening.

"I'm worried," he confided to Elias. "Debra doesn't seem to be feeling any better. It's five days, and after all her resting, she still insists she's tired."

"So, maybe she is."

"There's more. Every morning she runs straight to the bathroom. Even outside in the hallway, we can hear the wretching."

Elias made a face. "Has she seen a doctor?"

"Yussell is taking her to the clinic tomorrow."

Trying to reassure his friend, Elias put his arm around Shlomo. "I'm sure Debra will be just fine in a few days." Shlomo made no reply. In his short life, Shlomo Zusstovetch had buried two parents, both victims of the cholera epidemic. Understandably, his sister's fatigue and vomiting scared him.

All the next day, Elias worried about Debra, too. Coming over on the ship, he had listened to Morton Lieberman describe a long list of diseases. At the time, Elias had dismissed his Hebrew teacher's obsession with illness, but now as he thought back on the conversations, he tried to figure out what could be ailing Debra. By early evening, Elias's boyish imagination had gotten the best of him. As he rushed over to Adler's pharmacy to see his friend, he braced himself for catastrophe.

He ran up the back stairs to Debra's door. He took a deep breath before knocking; silently, he recited a prayer.

"Come in!"

Elias stepped inside and closed the door behind him. Then his jaw fell open. He couldn't stop gaping at the figure in front of him.

"Do you like it?" Debra asked hesitantly. She was blushing now and her bright pink cheeks made her look especially radiant. "My Yussell is so wonderful! He worked extra hours hammering and sawing away, just so his wife will look well-dressed in America." Debra twirled around to show off her new wig.

Except for those few moments on the ship when they first met, Elias had never seen Debra without a kerchief on her head. The wavy, dark brown wig, set in a fashionable style had indeed transformed the immigrant's appearance. Although Elias was thinking how lovely she looked, the first words out of his mouth were: "What happened at the doctor's?"

"How did you know about that?" she asked.

"Shlomo told me you haven't been feeling well. I was worried."

Debra lowered her eyes and smiled bashfully at the floor. "Thank you for your concern, but the doctor said there's no reason to be alarmed. All the symptoms are quite normal." The woman paused to look up at her friend. Her eyes were sparkling. "I'm expecting a child, Elias."

Now his face was beaming as well. "Mazel tov!" He then

recalled Lieberman's long list of dreaded diseases and burst out laughing.

"What's so funny?" asked Yussell as he came into the room and walked over to shake Elias's hand. Shlomo was just a step behind him.

"I've been worried about Debra since last night," Elias began.

Shlomo blushed. "The possibility of a baby never entered my mind," he said with a self-conscious giggle.

"Me neither," replied Elias. "This afternoon, all I could think about were all the disgusting diseases my uncle used to worry about on the ship. I figured it had to be one of them." The boy started laughing again. "I've actually discovered one condition that Morton Lieberman will never suffer."

11

Some Things Can't Be Mended

THE DAY OF the party finally arrived. As promised, Abe came for Elias in his horse and buggy. When the young tailor emerged from the side alley, Birenbaum could see the excitement in the boy's flushed face. His eyes glowed with anticipation. Underneath the shabby overcoat, Elias proudly wore his father's handsome blue suit, which he had made sure to mend in the shop after hours. Carefully, he climbed onto the carriage seat with a small package securely in his hand.

Birenbaum looked down and recognized the store's wrapping paper. He chuckled to himself. Of course, he had heard all about his employee's big night at the Pantages and how he had chosen to spend his winnings. At the moment, however, Birenbaum had something else on his mind.

"At services, Friday night, David Kaplan and I had a nice chat about your home in Gomel," he began.

Elias's stomach muscles tightened. The bright color in his cheeks was gone. "This is my home," he said defiantly.

"Of course," replied Birenbaum. "That's exactly why I'm so pleased my plan can proceed."

"What plan?"

"That's right. I haven't told you yet," the merchant answered with a coy grin. Hoping to create even more suspense, Birenbaum took a long pause while he steered the horse and buggy around the corner. Nervously, Elias bit down on his lower lip and waited.

Finally, Abe announced, "I've made arrangements for your parents and brother to leave Gomel. It is possible that they are on their way to Bremen as we speak."

"What?" shrieked Elias. "How? But where did Papa get the money?" Suddenly Elias understood. The boy was so excited that he was up on his feet.

"Sit down, son. We'll have an accident," laughed Birenbaum, and he explained how he had authorized Kaplan to make all the necessary arrangements. "That's why David had to ask you so many questions. But if all goes as planned," Birenbaum said proudly, "they should be able to sail from Bremen the first week in February. Of course, I've paid extra, so they shouldn't be herded into third class."

The boy was so choked up with emotion that for several seconds, all he could do was sit there struggling with his thoughts. Try as he might, he could not stop the stream of tears running down his face. Birenbaum simply patted his passenger on the knee.

"I'm glad I could help. You're a good son, but fourteen years old is just too young for a boy to shoulder the burden all alone."

Suddenly, Elias's eyes were wide open. "You haven't told

anyone else my age?" he demanded. Elias still worried that once his secret was revealed, the officials would come after him—or even worse, stop his parents from entering the country.

"Son, I promise you that no one will hear your secret from my lips. Now, get that frown off your face. I thought you were happy."

"I am! I am!" Elias shouted wildly.

"Good!" And in his fatherly fashion, Birenbaum patted the boy once more.

When they finally stopped in front of the three-story yellow house, Elias arched his neck to look up at the red slate roof. "This is yours?" Elias said in awe.

Birenbaum nodded proudly. If given the chance, he gladly would have told Elias about his own impoverished childhood, but their conversation ended abruptly.

From the parlor window, Rebecca had watched them arrive. She came running down the porch steps. The skirt of her blue taffeta party dress bounced in the breeze as she rushed toward Elias.

"Without a coat you come waltzing out here? Do you want to catch pneumonia?" the father shouted at his daughter.

"Oh, Papa" is all Rebecca said as she motioned for Elias to follow her into the house. Mrs. Whitehall was waiting at the door to take the boy's coat. But first he turned to Rebecca.

"This is for you," he said and handed her the birthday present.

Rebecca blushed. "Thank you. I read in the paper how you won first prize at the Theater. My father told me you spent your winnings on me. No matter what it is, I love it already."

Now Elias was blushing, too. "Open it."

Rebecca looked over at Mrs. Whitehall to make sure it was

proper to unwrap the gift so early. The housekeeper nodded her approval.

The music box delighted Rebecca. To show Elias her appreciation, she took the hand-painted figurine and set it as the centerpiece on the dining room table. "Now everyone will see it when we have our cake and ice cream."

Some classmates were at the door and Rebecca ran to greet them. She introduced Elias to all her friends, but after the first few minutes, they mostly ignored him. Elias didn't even notice. The news about his family had put him in such a state of ecstasy that nothing else mattered. He even had a big smile for Ethel Steinberg.

"Good afternoon, Elias," the woman said with surprise. "I didn't know you were invited." She made no effort to mask her disapproval as she rudely walked away from Elias. Luckily, Mrs. Whitehall appeared a second later.

"Cake will be served in the dining room," she announced after ringing a silver dinner bell.

Everyone found a place at the table. A girlfriend admired the figurine in the center. Then another reached out to examine the music box. Suddenly, everyone wanted to look at it. Rebecca agreed that it could be passed around slowly. "But be very careful," she warned them.

Rebecca had seated Elias next to her. After a bit of coaxing from the hostess, the boy agreed to tell the story about the Pantages. When he concluded, "So the next morning, I took my winnings and bought the music box," all the girls sighed.

"That's the sweetest thing I ever heard," someone squealed.

"I want to hear more about the ship," bellowed one of the boys. Suddenly, Elias was the center of attention. Ethel Steinberg was not pleased. Seated at the opposite end of the room, she acted completely indifferent when the figurine was handed to her. She didn't even bother to pass it along, but simply put it down next to her water glass.

The chatter and laughter around the table were at high pitch, when a crashing noise suddenly brought a hush to the room. All heads turned toward Ethel Steinberg.

In the course of conversation, the woman had been waving her arms about to make a point. By accident, her hand had knocked the porcelain figure into the water glass. The goblet shattered and the music box broke into several pieces. Ice water was dripping from the tablecloth.

"Oh, dear, look what a mess I've made," said Ethel, pushing her chair away from the wet tablecloth. "Mrs. Whitehall, please get me some napkins."

Rebecca cried, "Aunt Ethel, what have you done?"

"I'm sorry, dear. But it's just water. Nothing will be damaged."

"But look! My music box! It's ruined!"

"Oh, honey. How clumsy of me." The woman looked down on the table and for the first time realized the extent of the damage. Her tone was genuinely apologetic. "Don't worry. I'll buy you another just like it tomorrow. Abe, you do have another?"

"Of course," said Rebecca's father. "I'll put it away first thing in the morning." Knowing better than to make a fuss in front of a room full of guests, Rebecca did not mention the figurine again. Still, she managed to flash an angry frown at her aunt. The party resumed and no one seemed to give the accident a second thought. But once the guests adjourned into the parlor, Elias sneaked back into the dining room to separate the large china fragments from the broken glass. All of a sudden, the boy felt someone tapping him on the shoulder.

"Rebecca tells me you're quite handy at mending seams. Well, broken teacups and dishes are my specialty. Why don't you wait to see what I can do?"

The housekeeper was as good as her word. After most of the guests had departed, Rebecca pulled Elias into the library and led him to a corner of the room. She pointed to the dainty porcelain figure on the top shelf. It stood by a photograph of Frances Birenbaum.

"It will be safe up there," she said softly. Elias looked upward and studied the mother's picture.

"You look just like her," he said.

"Thank you!" Rebecca answered with a radiant smile. "And thanks again for such a beautiful birthday present."

Elias found himself staring into Rebecca's eyes. His face inched closer. Did he dare press his lips against hers?

"Becky, there you are!" a shrill voice called from outside the room. Rebecca snapped her head around. "Uncle Gus and I must be going. Come see us out, young lady."

Rebecca meekly followed Ethel Steinberg out of the room. Meanwhile, Elias plopped down into the big burgundy leather chair and kicked his long legs up on top of the matching ottoman. He glanced at the figurine on the shelf and started to whistle.

In his bed that night, Elias closed his eyes and tried to visualize those few precious seconds in the library. What a day! To think his parents would soon be in America and that he had almost kissed Rebecca Birenbaum.

The first thing on Monday morning, Joe and Izzy wanted to hear about the party. Elias described most of the afternoon in detail, but naturally omitted his brief encounter with Rebecca. He saved the news about his family for last.

The teenager's excitement was contagious. By the end of the work day, all the clerks in the department store were praising Mr. Birenbaum for his generosity.

"They'll be here before you know it," was the common response.

Debra, Shlomo, and Yussell also rejoiced. In fact, everyone at the Settlement House was whispering about Elias's good fortune. "What a lucky young man," Elias heard a group of immigrants gossiping among themselves.

"I wouldn't mind a rich benefactor like that Birenbaum," someone moaned wistfully. Elias shivered with excitement every time he thought about his good fortune.

Twelve days after the party, a clerk rushed into the shop. "The boss wants to see you in his office right away. Oh, and David Kaplan is here."

Elias swallowed hard. "Is this it? Are they on the ship? Did they leave Bremen?" he asked in one breath.

"Could be," the clerk said with a shrug before disappearing down the hall. Elias looked over at Joe.

"What are you waiting for? Are you glued to your chair or something? Go find out what the man wants," Joe ordered.

Elias ran to the staircase. His long legs stretched over three steps at a time. Birenbaum had left the door open and Elias rushed up to the desk without noticing Kaplan seated against the wall.

"You wanted to see me?" he asked, catching his breath.

Birenbaum studied the boy's hopeful expression. "Sit down, son," he said quietly.

While pulling up a chair, Elias looked over his shoulder and saw David Kaplan. "Hello, there," he greeted him.

"Hello, Elias." Elias turned his chair so that he would be facing both men.

"Well? When will they be here?" The suspense was almost painful.

Abe sighed. "I'm afraid the news is not good."

"What do you mean? They're still coming, aren't they?" Elias was back up on his feet.

"Please, Elias," Kaplan said while gesturing with his hand, "you really should sit down." Elias remained standing.

"Why? What's happened? What's going on here?"

Birenbaum came from around the back of his desk and put his arm around the boy's broad shoulders. He held him with a firm grip.

"We've just received word about a pogrom. A lot of people were killed." The boy's knees buckled under him and he collapsed back into the chair.

"It happened the day they were supposed to leave," explained Kaplan. "The Agent's report included a list of the victims. Your parents' names were among them."

At first Elias sat motionless. With tears trickling down his own face, Birenbaum knelt by the boy's side. His head hung down in misery. His effort had come too late.

Suddenly, Elias thought he must be suffocating. The heavy pain growing in his side felt as if someone were squeezing all the breath out of his lungs. He doubled over gasping for air.

"Get control of yourself," pleaded Kaplan, who was about to rush out for the doctor.

Elias sat upright with his head tilted back and his eyes closed. He was still breathing heavily. "You haven't mentioned my brother, Reuben."

"We think he's dead, too."

"But his name's not on the list?"

"No."

"Then we must find out," Elias demanded.

Birenbaum stood up and turned to David Kaplan. "Contact the agents in Galveston, New York, London—whoever can help. If that boy is alive, get him out of the country. I don't care what it costs."

Elias sat in his chair, shaking his head. "No," he said quietly. "I must go back for him myself."

"Don't be ridiculous! It's too dangerous," protested Birenbaum. "The agents are very capable. Let them handle it."

Too weak to argue, Elias just nodded.

That first week of mourning, Elias observed the Jewish tradition of "sitting shiva." He did not leave his apartment. Friends came to pay their respects and look after his needs.

Even afterward, the boy was not alone in his grief. Every morning and evening Joe, Izzy, Yussell, and Shlomo took turns meeting Elias at the orthodox synagogue, where the boy recited the mourner's prayer. Each night, Debra insisted he come back to their home for dinner. Rebecca visited Elias at the store as often as she could.

Even Ethel Steinberg poured out her love. When she was told of the tragedy, her eyes filled up with tears. "That poor young man," she said over and over again. Although she may not have wanted her niece to marry an immigrant, Ethel was still a champion of the less fortunate. Almost every day she put in his apartment pots of chicken soup, batches of chocolate-chip cookies, or loaves of freshly baked bread. "You must keep up your strength," she would tell him.

All the attention did not ease the boy's suffering and he kept telling Debra, "I'm going back for Reuben."

"Please, Elias," the young woman would beg him almost

every night, "give Mr. Birenbaum some time. It's been less than two weeks. You know it's better if they can locate him. Besides, what about money to sail back and forth—plus the fare for Reuben?"

"I'm hoping Mr. Birenbaum will give me a loan. I'll work it off when I come back." In his mind, Elias had figured it all out.

"But what if the immigration officials don't let you back into America? What if you return to Gomel and there's another pogrom? What if you contract cholera on the ship? What then?" Debra demanded.

The boy's eyes were welling up with tears. "I know what my parents would expect of me." He had never told anyone about his nightmare. The image of Reuben slipping off his shoulders and being swallowed up by the wild sea still haunted him.

Elias never imagined Birenbaum would refuse his request. "You know, son, it's not the money. I'll pay ten times the amount for an agent to find your brother. But I don't want you to go back there. Please be patient. I'm sure any day now we will hear word about Reuben."

But no word came.

12

The Journey Home

ANOTHER WEEK PASSED. An agent from Gomel finally telegrammed Kaplan.

> *This last pogrom was devastating. So many mutilated bodies still not identified.*

Birenbaum read the message and he could feel his bones chilling inside of him. He rubbed his hands together for warmth.

"This must not be repeated to a soul," he ordered Kaplan.

"What about Cherry?"

"Especially Elias. Until we have evidence one way or another, I expect the search to continue. Double your manpower if necessary. I'm good for the money."

Elias couldn't live with the uncertainty. The very day Birenbaum had ordered Kaplan to double his efforts, Elias went to Birenbaum's office and pleaded once more.

The merchant studied the sad figure before him. Even with all of Ethel's baskets of food, Elias had grown gaunt. The heavy circles under his eyes were very dark.

"No matter what you think, Mr. Birenbaum," Elias begged, "I must return!"

But the merchant refused to discuss the matter any further. "The agents will find out the truth. Now tell Izzy I said you should leave early this afternoon. I want you to see a doctor."

Elias had no intention of going to the clinic when he strolled out of the store that afternoon. While waiting at the corner to cross the street, he took Lieberman's gold watch out of his pocket to check the time. When he looked up, he saw Mrs. Steinberg walk into the hardware store. An idea occurred to him and he raced across the street with the watch still tucked away in his palm. This last month, Ethel Steinberg had often asked him if he needed money. Elias always declined the offer, but now he wanted her help.

When she saw him, her face lit up with a smile. "Oh good! I can give you this personally. I was going to leave it at your doorstep, but now you've saved me a trip upstairs." The woman handed him a tin of strudel.

"It smells delicious," Elias said politely. "But would you still come up to my apartment? We need to talk about something very important." Ethel Steinberg heard the urgency in the boy's voice and followed quietly. Once the door to the apartment was shut, Elias explained the situation.

"I know Mr. Birenbaum is doing what he thinks is right, and I understand that he's concerned for my safety. But Reuben is only six years old."

His voice quivered and the tears began to fall. Ethel Steinberg searched in her purse for a handkerchief. She handed it to Elias, and then looked for another to dry her own eyes.

"My brother-in-law has only the best of intentions," she sniffled, "but you're a man and must make your own decisions. I know if it were my baby brother, I'd be on the next boat no matter what. Just tell me how much you'll need."

Again, tears rolled down his face. "Thank you," he wept. "But I refuse to take any handouts."

"I understand. When you return, you can pay me back each week from your earnings."

"Yes. That's what I propose to do." Elias paused for a moment and then slowly opened the hand holding Lieberman's gold watch. "If something happens, at least you'll have this. It's solid gold; it's worth a lot of money."

Ethel Steinberg put her arms up to motion that she didn't want any collateral. "Now you sound like Abe. Of course, you'll come back."

Elias insisted, and Ethel put the watch in her pocketbook. She promised he would have enough money the next day.

"Another thing," Elias reminded Ethel as she turned to leave. "I don't want anyone to know that I'm going. You've got to keep this a secret."

For the next several days, Elias made a special effort to pay extra attention to all the clerks in the store, Joe and Izzy, friendly customers, friends from the Settlement House, his teacher, Miss Goldstein, and even David Kaplan. That Sunday afternoon, he planned a surprise visit.

"My father's not home," said Rebecca who was flustered to see the boy on her front porch.

"I came to see you," he smiled.

For almost two hours, Elias and Rebecca sat and talked in the library. In that time Elias forgot his own troubles and entertained Rebecca with funny stories about his father's customers in Gomel, Morton Lieberman, the sailors on the ship, and whatever he thought might make the beautiful girl sitting next to him smile. Rebecca had a deep belly laugh and it was contagious. Mrs. Whitehall heard the laughter all the way in the kitchen and started smiling herself.

Rebecca begged Elias to stay for dinner, but he had already made other plans. Before walking out of the library he pointed up at the music box.

"Still looks safe up there," he commented.

"Don't worry," said Rebecca. "I'll never let anything happen to it again."

Elias paused at the French doors and looked around the library.

"Is something wrong?" Rebecca asked.

"No, no, no," mumbled Elias, who was just wondering whether he would ever see such a world of luxury again.

Rebecca walked him outside to the front porch. As usual, she hadn't bothered to put on a coat and stood there shivering.

"Maybe you can come next Sunday for dinner," she said with chattering teeth.

"Maybe" was all Elias replied. Although he had a slight smile on his face, his eyes could not hide the sadness. Rebecca grabbed his hand and squeezed it. Then suddenly she stood up on her tiptoes and kissed him on the cheek.

"Come back, Elias Cherevnosky," she yelled, running into the house.

From Rebecca's, Elias went to Debra's. Again, he seemed to forget his troubles. He, Yussell, and Shlomo joked until late in the evening. Before he left, Elias made a special point to hug his friends.

"What is this? You act as if you're leaving on a long trip," Shlomo said.

"Don't be ridiculous!" Elias answered quickly, mimicking his boss's favorite phrase.

"Well then, I'll see you tomorrow night in class."

"And don't forget!" added Yussell. "Plan to stay late. The newcomers are arriving from Galveston. David Kaplan and Mr. Billikopf would like as many of us as possible to welcome them."

"You know," boasted Shlomo. "It's nice to know that *we're* no longer the 'greenhorns.'"

"I'm afraid we still have a long way to go," chuckled Yussell.

"Not all of us," argued Debra, and she looked down at her belly which was beginning to protrude ever so slightly. "This one is all American."

It was past midnight when Debra walked Elias to the door. She stepped outside with him. "Debra, go back! You don't dare catch a cold now."

"Oh, so you're going to order me around too," she groaned. "Well, all right. I'll see you tomorrow night."

"I don't think so," Elias confessed. "Joe has invited me for dinner." He hated lying to Debra, but he knew there was no other way.

"Maybe you can come afterward. Remember, Mr. Billikopf is counting on us."

"I can't," he said softly.

"Why not?" she persisted.

"I just can't, Debra," he snapped back at her. Elias saw the hurt look on her face and heaved a sigh of frustration.

"Please understand. My parents would have been on that

ship. I can't greet those other people. It's still too painful." He ran down the stairs.

From her bedroom window, Debra watched Elias walk back to the hardware store. When she turned to give Yussell a kiss good night, her tears fell on his cheek.

In the store the next day, no one suspected a thing. At five minutes to six, Elias folded his last pair of trousers and carefully put everything in order. When he was sure Joe and Izzy weren't looking, he slipped a sealed envelope into his sewing box. It was a note for Rebecca. He had written only two sentences: "I hope this is not good-bye. I won't forget you."

The train to Galveston was scheduled to depart at 7:20 P.M. Elias walked into the station at 6:30. He hadn't anticipated a long line at the ticket counter and stood there tapping his foot. He looked around at the busy station and was reminded of his first day in Kansas City.

"What luck to have met Mr. Scott on the train," he had often thought. But in one of his letters, Jacob Cherevnosky had corrected his son. "It is never luck, boychik. These things are planned from above." Elias lifted his eyes upward and wondered if someone was waiting for him this time.

These last two weeks he had been so adamant about going home for Reuben that no one would have suspected the terror inside him. He knew firsthand the perils that lay ahead. But truly a man now, Elias did not waver as he stepped up to the window.

"One for Galveston."

The depot wasn't the only place buzzing that night. In preparation for the new immigrants' arrival, the Settlement House was swarming with people. Classes had been canceled and folks were either hanging decorations, carrying tables and chairs, or arranging platters of food. Naturally,

Ethel Steinberg was present. Her ladies' auxiliary was providing the punch and cookies. Even Gus and Abe had promised to stop by after work.

Expecting to spend most of the time with Elias, Rebecca had gladly accompanied her aunt. When Debra told her that Elias had made other plans for the night, Rebecca didn't even try to hide her disappointment. Before she could pull her father out of the dining hall, David Kaplan ran into the room to announce that the coach of immigrants was just pulling up to the Settlement House. In all the commotion, Debra felt faint. Yussell insisted she leave immediately and both he and Shlomo escorted her home. Once outside in the fresh air, Debra felt fine and as soon as she was tucked in bed for the night, she insisted Shlomo return for the celebration.

Songs, toasts, and pledges of friendship welcomed the strangers. The travel-weary immigrants wept with joy. As was her custom, Ethel Steinberg greeted everyone personally.

She was leaning over to welcome a young child who was gripping the hand of an older gentleman when someone accidently pushed her from behind. The woman lost her footing and dropped her purse.

"Oh dear," she cried when she saw her crocheted handbag on the floor.

The child politely bent down and handed it to her.

"Thank you," she said while rummaging through the handbag. "I just hope it didn't break." Ethel pulled out the gold pocket watch and checked the crystal face. Then she wound it gently and held it up to her ear to make sure the timepiece was still ticking. "I've been carrying this around for days. I've got to remember to put it someplace safe."

The small boy's chaperone saw the watch and grabbed it from her hand. "How did you get my pocket watch?" he demanded in Yiddish. "Who are you? What are you doing with my solid gold watch?"

"I beg your pardon," cried Ethel. "This most certainly does not belong to you," and she snatched it back again.

"Thief! Thief!" the man shouted wildly. Heads turned. Rebecca and her father heard the commotion just as Gus began to pull Abe by the arm.

"Ethel's in the middle of that ruckus." The three of them made their way through the crowd.

"Gus, this man is a lunatic! He insists the gold pocket watch is his." Ethel Steinberg raised the timepiece high in the air above the short man's reach.

Rebecca stretched her head backward. "That belongs to—"

"I know perfectly well to whom it belongs, young lady," snapped the aunt.

"Ethel, what are you doing with someone else's watch?" asked Gus.

Ethel Steinberg hesitated. "It's a long story, sweetheart. I'll tell you later."

"Lady, give me my watch!" The little man pounded his feet on the floor and the crowd grew around him. When Shlomo strolled back into the dining room, he squeezed through the onlookers to see what was happening.

"Mr. Lieberman, I can't believe it's you."

"Shlomo, tell this crazy woman to give me back my watch. Then take me to Elias," he barked.

Ethel gasped. "Elias Cherry? How do you know Elias?"

"This is his Uncle Morton," Shlomo boomed.

"Oh no! What have I done?" Ethel blurted out the entire story. Minutes later Birenbaum was in his carriage, heading for the train station.

"Wait for us," Shlomo cried. Lieberman was huffing and

puffing with a frightened little boy named Reuben Cherevnosky by his side. All three climbed into the carriage.

"Get out of the way," Birenbaum yelled down Independence Avenue. His horse stopped for no one.

"All aboard! Track 2 for Galveston, Texas," the conductor was calling from the platform. Elias stepped onto the train and took an empty place next to the window. The boy leaned his head back against the leather seat and closed his eyes.

All of sudden he heard a tapping sound. Elias tried to ignore it and twisted his head toward the other side of the seat. The noise grew louder. He turned his head back to the glass. In a split second, Elias Cherry was on his feet and pushing his way through the mob of boarding passengers. He just made it to the open door when he felt the train wheels begin to roll along the tracks. Clutching his bag to his chest, he jumped off the train.

Birenbaum ran over to the boy. "Are you all right?"

Elias couldn't speak. He just stood there staring at Reuben sitting on top of Shlomo's shoulders.

"I'm here!" the child squealed in Yiddish. He was waving his tiny hand in the air.

Lieberman put his arms around Elias and wept into his shoulder. "I didn't think this day would ever come. I'm so sorry about Jacob and Dena. Oh, they were so proud of you and so happy when they received the tickets to come to America. Those murderers killed everyone in sight." Lieberman stepped back to compose himself. He blew his nose, but the tears never stopped.

"I was already at the station. When I heard the horses, I rolled into a ditch. I never expected to live. Afterward, I went back for everyone. Your father's shop was rubble. Little

Reuben was hiding between two bolts of cloth. What else is there to say? We took the next train for Bremen."

Elias held his little brother in his arms as they walked out to the carriage. Mr. Lieberman sat next to Birenbaum. Reuben sat in between Elias and Shlomo and snuggled up to his brother. The horse trotted at a steady pace.

Reuben, who had been too scared to cry or complain these last weeks, suddenly burst into tears. "I'm cold and hungry," he wailed. "I want Mama and Papa."

Me too, thought Elias. He saw that Reuben's neck was exposed to the windy night. He took off his red scarf and wrapped it around him.

"Shh, boychik," Elias comforted his brother.

For a long time, no one spoke. Then they turned the corner. Elias tugged at the little boy's sleeve and pointed to the street sign.

"Look, Reuben!" he whispered into his brother's ear. "We're home."